For Sam

First American edition published in 2003 by Carolrhoda Books, Inc.

Published by arrangement with Flyways, an imprint of Floris Books

Copyright © 2001 by Steve Alton

Carolrhoda Books, Inc.
A division of Lerner Publishing Group
241 First Avenue North
Minneapolis, MN 55401 U.S.A.

Website address: www.lernerbooks.com

Library of Congress Cataloging-in-Publication Data

Alton, Steve.
    The Malifex / by Steve Alton.
        p.   cm.
    Summary: In the Dorset, England, countryside on a family vacation, a video game fanatic reluctantly embarks on a quest to battle an ancient evil, aided by the daughter of a Wiccan and a man once apprenticed to Merlin.
    ISBN: 0–8225–0959–8 (lib. bdg. : alk. paper)
    [1. Magic—Fiction. 2. Wizards—Fiction. 3. Witches—Fiction. 4. Adventure and adventurers—Fiction. 5. England—Fiction.] I. Title.
PZ7.A466 Mal 2003
[Fic]—dc21   2001008651

Manufactured in the Unites States of America
1 2 3 4 5 6 –SB– 08 07 06 05 04 03

the Malifex

STEVE ALTON

Carolrhoda Books, Inc. • Minneapolis

author's note

"The Song of Amergin" is a very early piece of verse, supposedly uttered by Amergin, bard and chieftain of the Milesians, as he first set foot in Ireland. The Milesians, according to legend, were a Gaelic tribe who invaded Ireland from Spain, displacing the original inhabitants, the Tuatha de Danaan.

Much of the background information about the religion of Wicca comes from a number of excellent websites maintained by members of the international Wiccan community, and from the books of Janet and Stewart Farrar.

> I am the wind upon the sea
> I am the flood across the plain
> I am the hawk above the cliff
> I am the thorn beneath the rose
> I am the stag of seven tines
> I am the salmon in the pool
> I am wisdom; who but I
> cools the head aflame with smoke?
>
> I am the hills where poets walk
> I am the lure from beyond world's end
> I am the spear that rears for blood
> I am the tear the sun lets fall
> I am the breaker, threatening doom
> I am an infant; who but I
> peeps from the unknown dolmen arch?

From *The Song of Amergin*, Celtic Traditional

the beginning

The wind, rising up the long flank of the hill, hissed through the short grass as the procession of figures emerged from the trees. They strode in single file to the hill's summit, then turned to the east, into the teeth of the gale. The leading figure, tall and robed in white, was forced to lean into the wind, supporting himself on a wooden staff. At the tip of the staff, higher than his head, a sphere of blue light crackled and spat.

The long, sinuous ridge along which the procession walked was flat-topped and bare, a bleak place of flint-studded turf and stunted bushes. The train of robed figures looked tiny beneath the vastness of the night sky, where tattered rags of cloud were hurled across the face of a full moon, and stars glittered, cold and bright.

After a mile of hard walking, the leader came to a halt before a low structure of stone slabs. His companions gathered around him, forming a loose semicircle at the narrow end of the structure. By the light of his staff, he began to speak. As they were uttered, his words were whipped away in puffs of vapor on the wind. His speech concluded, he gestured to one of the assembled group, a man with a haunted look in his eyes. Looking around forlornly, the man stepped forward. One of his companions patted him on the shoulder as he passed. Great stone doors stood open at the end of the low building; the white-robed figure walked through them into the dark interior. With one last look around him, the man followed.

Some minutes later, the leader emerged, alone. With a look of great sadness, he spoke one word that closed the stone doors with a hollow boom. Then he turned, his white hair streaming behind him in the wind, and led the procession away.

chapter 1

Things were not looking good. He'd already missed one power-up opportunity, and he would need all the health bonuses he could get if he was to stand any chance against the level boss. He ducked around a corner, fired off a couple of shots, and dived sideways to pick up an armor bonus. The problem was, the steady swish of the windshield wipers and the drone of the car's engine were almost hypnotic, and his concentration was starting to slip. The headlights of the occasional passing car glared off the screen, making his eyes hurt, but after several hours of battling his way through the same level, there was no way he was going to give in now.

Poised for a particularly tricky maneuver, he suddenly found himself flung toward the back of the passenger seat, the seat belt tight across his chest. The handheld computer game fell to the floor and bounced under his father's seat as he braced both hands in front of him.

"What is it, Paul?" Sam heard his mother ask in a strange voice.

Peering around his mother's headrest, he had a clear view of what had caused his father to brake so hard. In the middle of the road in front of them was a dark shape, the size of a large dog. It remained motionless for several seconds, staring into the car, before turning and padding swiftly into the long grass that lined the road. As it turned, its eyes flared green for a moment in the car's headlights.

"I don't know," replied his father hesitantly. "It looked like—well, you could see what it looked like—a big black cat, but I've never seen a cat that big."

"It's dark, Paul. It's difficult to judge the size of things in the dark. It could have been a dog," said his mother, but her voice held a note of uncertainty.

"It's the Beast of Bodmin!" Sam piped up from the back. "I've seen it on TV!"

"Sam, Bodmin is in Cornwall; this is Dorset. Anyway, like your mother says, it was probably just a dog. Everyone okay?" His father looked at each of them in turn. They nodded. "Okay. Let's get going. It can't be far now."

As the car plunged once more into the tunnel of dark lanes, Sam settled back into his seat and closed his eyes. The screen of the video game, lying under his father's seat, was blank. The game was long since over. "All those hours of effort for nothing," he thought. "I hope it's not going to be another one of those vacations."

The next morning, Sam awoke in a strange bed and experienced the moment of confusion that comes when waking in new surroundings. Rubbing his eyes, he looked around the room—floral curtains; another bed, unused, next to his own; a scattering of cheap, framed prints depicting local landmarks; and a battered chest of drawers.

The memory of their arrival the previous night began to return: his father collecting the cottage key from the farmhouse; staggering from the car with suitcases; the hasty assignment of rooms; and then to bed, barely able to stay awake. And the memory came, too, of a dark feline shape in the glare of the headlights—a flash of green eyes.

Sam stretched against the feel of strange sheets. "The Beast of Bodmin," he thought, "definitely." There had been a bunch of such sightings across southern England in recent years and not just on Bodmin Moor. Sam remembered a documentary, full of shaky, amateur videotapes of obviously feline black shapes, but with no sense of scale. Most of the experts were adamant that these sightings were of nothing more than large tomcats, but some people maintained—and Sam was willing to believe them—that there was something more unusual out there. And now Sam had seen it with his own eyes.

"The Beast of Bodmin. Cool!"

Rolling over, he noticed the feeble glow of light from the curtains, suggesting it was still very early. "Just my luck," he thought, "first day of vacation and awake at the crack of dawn." Hearing a strange noise, he pulled open the curtains a little and peered out. "Oh, great! Absolutely terrific!" he thought. A long row of black-and-white backs was making its way along the track below his window, steaming in the cold morning air. "Cows. This is the countryside. I'm going to get woken up every morning at the crack of dawn by cows. And tractors, I bet. And guys with straw in their mouths shouting 'Ooooaaaaar!'" At this thought, he got the giggles, to which he was prone from time to time, and he lay there for a while grinning to himself.

"Sam? Are you awake?" called his mother. "Breakfast!" So his parents were awake, too. No chance of going back to sleep. This could get serious if it continued for the entire week. He made it a rule, when on vacation, to try and stay in bed until midday if possible.

He threw on a pair of old jeans and a T-shirt and paused in front of the full-length mirror behind the door. He tried to plaster down a tuft of hair that had sculpted itself into a weird shape during the night, but it continued to defy the forces of gravity. He shrugged, made a face at his reflection, then made his way down the twisting wooden stairs to the big stone-floored kitchen, where his nose told him bacon was cooking.

The cottage was, in fact, no such thing. It had been an outbuilding of the farm, probably a barn of some kind, and had been converted, like so many such buildings, into a vacation rental. It had been converted well, though, with parts salvaged from other old properties. Everything looked very authentic and cottagey, right down to the woodworm holes.

"Help yourself to bacon and eggs," announced his mother, looking up as he walked into the kitchen. "The eggs are fresh. One of the local girls dropped them off this morning as a welcome present. She must be about your age."

"Don't, Mom." Sam sighed, helping himself from the frying pan.

"It would do you good to meet someone your own age, someone to talk to," his mother continued.

"But she's a girl!" Sam exclaimed in disgust.

"He's right, you know," chimed in his father from the breakfast table. "Better hang some garlic over the doors and windows!"

"He spends too much time staring at that stupid video game, Paul. It would do him good to get out in the fresh air with someone his own age." This was a frequent theme of his mother's.

"Yes, but a girl, honey? Can't be too careful with girls. I mean, I met you, and look where it got me!"

"Oh, I swear you two are as bad as each other. I'm going to get dressed. Sam, be sure and have some breakfast. Your father will no doubt drag us all over Dorset today."

His father, in keeping with vacation tradition, was surrounded by the kind of leaflets and brochures that always seem to be found in rental cottages—advertisements for adventure playgrounds, stately homes, various museums. It was his father's task, and had been on every family vacation Sam could remember, to analyze these leaflets and come up with a program of entertainment for the family. It was also traditional for the rest of the family to be deeply dissatisfied with the entertainment provided for them, although they never, of course, offered any alternative suggestions.

"Anything you like here, Son?" asked his father, as Sam sat down at the table with a plate of bacon and eggs.

"Dunno. Don't care, really. Whatever."

"Don't bowl me over with your enthusiasm. What about the tank museum?"

"Okay. Sounds . . . interesting. Do you get to drive one?" he asked around a mouthful of toast and egg white.

"I doubt they would let you loose with a tank," his father replied with a smile. "Anyway, we'll pencil it in for a rainy day, because it looks like it's mostly indoors."

As his father returned to his leaflets, Sam drifted in thought. A tank museum, huh? So that was to be the highlight of this vacation? Tanks were okay, he'd played a few computer games where he'd had to drive a tank, but a bunch of old machines gathering dust in some hangar? Museums of any kind, no matter how interesting the subject, made him antsy. There was something stifling about them, something about an interesting subject pinned down and frozen for the public to gawk at. Sam much preferred to participate, to be a player rather than a spectator.

Apart from sports, of course. He hated sports with a passion and sucked at most organized games. He carefully cultivated a contagious skin condition to avoid swimming and usually had to face the ritual humiliation of being the last to be picked for any team. That, and his generally lanky build—he was several inches taller than his classmates—should have made him a total outcast. His one redeeming feature, however, was his skill with computer games. He was tolerated as a prime source of hints, tips, and cheat codes. It didn't hurt that his generous allowance enabled him to buy a steady stream of the latest games.

After breakfast, Sam helped his father load the car with the usual equipment for a family day out: hiking boots, parkas, extra sweaters. It looked as though the parkas would definitely be needed, too. A thick mist—as wet as a light shower of rain—was spilling down from the hills behind the farm. They drove down the farm track, which brought them to a minor road that eventually became the main street of Brenscombe, the nearest village. Sam looked up briefly from his computer game and noted without much interest a huddle of stone cottages, a squat stone church, and a scattering of small shops, all soon left behind.

Their destination for the day was Swanage, a seaside town that lay on the coast some three miles to the east. Despite the heavy drizzle, Swanage turned out to be pleasant enough, less tacky than most such places, although not without its share of amusement arcades and souvenir shops. At the top of the main street was a station, which, they discovered, formed one end of a restored steam railroad line, but no trains were in evidence. Sam's father filed it away as another possible activity for a rainy day, although Sam wasn't sure how much wetter it would have to get to qualify!

Having exhausted the entertainment potential of Swanage, they piled back into the car and headed west of town to Durleston Country Park. Here, they put on hiking boots and parkas in an almost deserted parking lot and set off for a walk along the clifftops. His father read out the names of features of interest that they passed along the coast—Dancing Ledge, Tilly Whim Caves, Blackers Hole—but there was little to be seen in the gray light and increasingly heavy rain.

Sam thrust his hands deep into the pockets of his parka, but the rain trickled down his arms and collected in his pockets. His earlier premonition had been right—this was going to be one of those vacations! Another in a long succession of such vacations. Oh, for a warm bedroom, a vast supply of chips and salsa, and a computer game! The thought made him feel even colder, causing him to shiver, sending a cascade of rainwater down his face from the rim of his hood.

Soon, even his father agreed that the weather was unsuitable, and they turned back. By now it was midafternoon, and the family's spirits were low. Not daring to suggest another outdoor activity, Sam's father said, "Tell you what, let's go back to base, dry off, and then think about what to do next." This idea won total agreement. They walked gratefully back to the parking lot, put their dripping clothes in the trunk, and climbed into the car, which steamed gently as the heater went to work. The windshield wipers swished monotonously, and Sam settled back with his computer game, glad to be warm and dry.

Back at the cottage, with a log fire burning in the hearth, even Sam's father lost his enthusiasm for a return to the great outdoors. "Maybe we should call it a day. Don't want to overdo it." Sam and his mother exchanged a glance of mutual relief.

"I know!" exclaimed his father. "How about a game of charades?" Sam groaned inwardly. Playing charades was one of the more painful ordeals that his parents inflicted on him. He found standing up in front of an audience, even an audience made up of his own parents, toe-curlingly embarrassing. This called for drastic action. Since it was still light out and seemed to have stopped raining, he asked, "Can I go and have a look around the farm?"

"Well, wrap up warm," said his mother, "and don't go anywhere you shouldn't. And close the gates behind you."

"Yes, Mom," Sam sighed.

"And be back before it gets dark."

"Yes, Mom!"

Pulling on a jacket, Sam escaped into the farmyard, relishing the prospect of his own company. Their cottage faced a group of low outbuildings across a cobbled yard, with cobwebbed windows and sagging tiled roofs. At one end of the yard, the track crossed a cattle grid and wound off toward the road. At the other, there was a gate into the grounds of the farm itself. A battered wooden sign announced "Woolgarston Farm." Remembering his mother's warning about not going where he shouldn't, he wandered to the gate and peered over.

The farmhouse was a solid, square building made of weathered golden stone, with a red-tiled roof. The yard showed evidence of the regular passage of cows, and their smell clung to everything. The kind of unidentifiable, rusting machinery found in farms everywhere littered the corners of the yard and peeped from under tarps in the sheds. Here and there, hens scratched in the disintegrating remains of hay bales.

On the far side of the farmyard was another gate and a glimpse of fields beyond. To his right, facing the farmhouse was a low cottage, an older version of the one in which Sam and his family were staying. Lights were visible inside the house, and a plume of white smoke rose from the chimney. A strange wall plaque—a green, ceramic face with leaves emerging from its nose and mouth—peered back at him from the wall near the door. Although its expression was neutral, almost friendly, Sam felt a shudder begin at the base of his spine and crawl up his back.

There were no other signs of life anywhere on the farm, so Sam figured it would be all right if he crossed the farmyard to the opposite gate and took a look at the fields beyond. He unlatched the gate, remembering to close it behind him, and slipped quietly across the yard. Reaching the far side, he stopped and glanced around. There still was no sign of anyone, so he climbed onto the bottom rail of the gate and hooked his elbows over the top, resting his chin on his hands. Before him, a field of lush grass rolled away to a hedge, a dark line in the distance. His eyes followed the hedge upward, to the lower slopes of the hill that loomed above the farm. As he stared at the shadowy bulk of the ridge, indistinct in the mist and twilight, the hairs on the back of his neck began to prickle. He shuddered and looked quickly away.

Gazing out over the misty fields, his mind began to wander. How on earth was he going to survive a whole week of early mornings, brisk walks in the mist and rain, and the steady assault of stately homes and tiny museums? If only he could persuade his parents to let him stay back at the cottage with his video games. But there was no hope of that—they strongly disapproved of his love of solitude and inactivity. The next five days were looking pretty grim.

Suddenly, something tapped him sharply on the shoulder. Sam's heart leaped in his throat. Spinning around, he was confronted by the grinning face of a girl, roughly his own age. She wore a quilted, green, sleeveless jacket, old jeans, and Wellington boots. Her reddish brown hair was pulled back into a single, long braid that hung down to the small of her back. Her skin was pale, but her cheeks were flushed with pink from the cold evening air.

"You sure jumped!" she crowed, obviously delighted. "My name's Charly. What are you doing?"

"Charly?" he replied with a scowl. "That's a boy's name."

"Yeah, yeah, yeah. Never heard that before. It's short for Charlotte, but don't even think about calling me that. Anyway, you didn't answer my question. What are you doing?"

"Nothing," replied Sam, avoiding her eyes, "Just looking at the view."

Charly gave him a knowing smile. "You're from the cottage, aren't you? People staying at the cottage always wander around. Did you enjoy your eggs this morning?"

"Huh?" Sam was confused for a moment. "Oh, that was you? Yes. Uh, thanks."

"Good. I might bring you some more in the morning." With that, Charly turned and strode off toward the nearby cottage. There was a brief glow of yellow light as she let herself in through the front door.

"Just great," thought Sam, "and Mom wanted me to get to know her? No way!" But then, as he walked back across the farmyard, the beginnings of a thought occurred to him. His parents would never let him hang around the cottage on his own while they went off for the day, but if they thought he had made a new friend. . . . Hmmmmm, this Charly could turn out to be useful after all.

18

He closed the farmyard gate and turned down the path to the front door of the rental cottage.

Across the farm track, in the darkness of the bushes, a pair of cold, green eyes watched the door close behind him.

chapter 2

The next morning, woken again by the cows on their way to be milked, Sam took the unusual step of jumping out of bed without being nagged, much to the surprise of his parents. He was anxious to put his plan into action, and it was essential that he was up and dressed as soon as possible. He was down in the kitchen a few minutes after his mother, and when he heard a knock at the door he jumped up from his seat at the breakfast table.

"I'll get it, Mom," he shouted, already on his way. As he had hoped, it was Charly.

"Oh, hello," she said, looking mildly amused as he flung open the front door. "I was just going to collect some eggs, wondered if you wanted any?"

"Who is it, Sam?" called his mother, wandering through into the hallway. "Oh, hello again."

"Charly just wanted to know if we wanted more eggs, Mom," Sam explained.

"Oh, that's all right, dear," she smiled at Charly. "We can't keep taking eggs from you."

"It's no problem," replied Charly. "We usually have more than we know what to do with."

"Perhaps I could help, Mom?" suggested Sam, risking a

nervous glance at Charly. She continued to look amused.

"Well, if Charly doesn't mind . . . ?" his mother began.

"No, I'd be glad to have the company," Charly replied. "Bring a coat. It's cold out."

Sam grabbed a coat from the pegs in the hallway and ran after Charly's retreating back, leaving his bewildered mother to close the door behind him.

"So, what brought this on?" Charly said with a hint of sarcasm as he caught up with her.

"Dunno, just never been on a farm before," replied Sam, feeling distinctly uncomfortable now that his plan was under way.

"Well, it's not that interesting, really, but we can have a look around if you like."

"Okay, that would be . . . er . . . nice," replied Sam, cringing inside. "Nice!" he thought. "I'm going to have to do better than 'nice!'"

They were in the yard outside the farmhouse, heading toward the outbuildings.

"The hens have their own henhouse," Charly explained, "but they wander all over the place, so you have to search to find all the eggs."

"Does your dad just keep cows and hens?" asked Sam, desperately trying to think of something to talk about.

"My dad? I haven't got a dad. Well, I have, obviously, but he's not around. This is Uncle Pete's farm. He lets me and my mom live in the old cottage over there. And yes, he mainly keeps dairy cattle. The hens are just for the family's use."

"So, what happened to your dad?" Sam asked, with

growing confidence. Making conversation wasn't that hard after all.

Charly stopped and stared at him for a moment.

"He left us, okay?" she said coldly, then turned and walked off. Sam cursed inwardly before running after her.

"Here we go," said Charly when Sam caught up with her. She seemed to have forgiven his moment of tactlessness.

They had stopped at an old hay bale, half-collapsed into an untidy pile that a hen had obviously used as a nest.

"Dive in," instructed Charly. Sam scooped up a couple of the eggs.

"Ugh, gross!" he shouted, dropping them back into the hay.

"What's the matter?" asked Charly.

"They're all covered in crud and stuff!"

"Yes, well they have been up a chicken's . . . well, use your imagination. You're in the country now, city boy—we have lots of crud and stuff!"

"I suppose so," said Sam, looking rather sheepish. "I'm just used to eggs coming in egg cartons from the supermarket."

Sam gritted his teeth and gingerly picked up the occasional egg, finding perhaps one egg for every five that Charly collected. After half an hour's work, they'd filled Charly's basket and went back to Sam's cottage.

"So, what else do you do around here?" asked Sam, "I mean, apart from collecting eggs?"

"Well, I help my uncle with things, with the milking and so on, and sometimes I help Mom, but I'm pretty much free to do what I want. I go exploring mostly, up on Brenscombe Hill." She gestured behind her, to the hill rising behind the farm. It promised to be a clearer day, the early patches of mist fading as the sun rose, and Sam could see that the hill stretched off in either direction from the farm, curving slightly at its farthest ends as it was lost to sight in the haze.

"It looks like a strange hill," he said after a moment.

"It is. It's a very special hill. It forms the Isle of Purbeck," replied Charly.

"How do you mean? We aren't on an island."

"Yes we are, sort of," said Charly. "This part of Dorset, Purbeck, is cut off from the rest by this hill. It's like a long, curved sausage running from coast to coast. The only gaps are at Corfe, where Corfe Castle is, and over toward Swanage. So this is a sort-of island—the Isle of Purbeck."

"You know a lot about it," Sam said, impressed.

"Well, like I said, it's special. It's a special place."

"Do you . . . er . . . could you show me some of the places you explore?" asked Sam, turning red around the ears.

"Hmmm . . . well, I suppose we could go up the hill." Charly didn't sound convinced, and Sam couldn't blame her. Even he wasn't convinced. Why should she go out of her way for somebody she had only met the previous day, trespassing on her uncle's property? "Yes, why not?" Charly said, almost to herself. "I haven't been for a while. Won't your parents mind?"

"Oh, no," answered Sam quickly. "I hope," he added to himself.

Later, after a breakfast of scrambled eggs—Sam tried not

to think about where they had come from—the conversation turned to the day's activities. Sam's father was heartened by the change in the weather and had come up with an itinerary of brisk country walks.

"Speaking of walks," began Sam, "Charly offered to show me around the farm and maybe to go and have a look at the hill behind here."

"Ah, young love!" chortled his father. "Reminds me of your mother and me."

"You were twenty-six when we met; don't tease the boy. Are you sure?" asked his mother, looking doubtfully at Sam. "I don't want you being a nuisance or wandering all over the countryside. What will you do for lunch?"

Sam hadn't thought of that. "Er . . . I could make some sandwiches for later."

"Well, I suppose, but don't go wandering too far. And wrap up warm. And don't be a nuisance."

"Mo-om! I'll be fine. Anyway, you're always saying you want me to make friends, get out more," complained Sam.

"Yes," admitted his mother, "but it all seems so, well, out of character."

Sam hurried off to prepare a packed lunch. When he had gone, his father peered over the top of his map, one eyebrow raised.

"I know," replied Sam's mother to the unspoken question, "it does seem odd. I hope he'll be all right."

"He'll be fine, honey—stop worrying about him. After all," he returned to his map, "what could happen to him out here?"

After further fussing and lots of instructions, Sam's

parents set off for the day, leaving him in the company of Charly. When the car had disappeared out of sight through the farm gate, Charly said, "Well, what would you like to do first?"

"Look," said Sam, "let's get a few things straight. I don't really like the countryside. I don't like fresh air, I don't like hills, and I don't really want to go off wandering about with . . . well . . . with girls. Sorry. It's nothing personal. I just wanted some time to myself. I've got sandwiches, I've got a computer game that I might, just might, eventually finish, and I've got my parents out of my hair. Now, you can go and do whatever it is you do, chase chickens or whatever, and I'll go and do what I do, and, when my parents get back, I'll tell them what a great time we had. Okay?"

Charly was staring at him with her mouth open. "Oh, I see," she said, turning pale with anger. "So, all that, that . . . interest, all those questions, all that was just to get your parents out of the way? You were just using me?"

Sam was starting to think he might have mishandled things. "Look, I'm sorry. This is a really nice place. Really. And I am interested. It's just, well, I don't do countryside. I just want to be left alone."

"Oh, you'll be left alone all right, you . . . you . . . oh!" Charly turned and stormed away, breaking into a run as she crossed the farmyard.

By now, Sam was almost convinced that he could have handled things better. He stared after Charly for a few moments, then returned to the cottage.

He retired to his bedroom and sat on the bed, but he found it difficult to concentrate on his video game. After the aliens had killed him for the third time, he gave up and threw the game on the bed in disgust. He was forced to admit to himself that he'd made a serious tactical error. If Charly was supposed to be his excuse for the rest of his vacation, then upsetting her on the second day had definitely been a bad move. More than that, Sam had an uneasy feeling that what he had done had been wrong. Unfair. He decided to try to smooth things over with Charly, although he thought it was possible she might never speak to him again. With a sigh, he put his video game back on the bedside table and headed for the farmyard.

On the far side of the yard, Sam saw Charly emerging from the cottage with a small backpack over her shoulder.

"Charly!" he shouted as she headed across the yard. She didn't even look around. Sam let himself through the gate and ran after her. "Charly! Wait!" he shouted again, waving frantically. He caught up with her on a path he hadn't noticed before, which led down the far side of the farmhouse, between the garden and an overgrown hedge. Charly continued to walk briskly away from him. Half-jogging to keep up, Sam tapped her on the shoulder. Suddenly, she spun around.

"Don't touch me!" Her eyes were red, as if she had been crying. "Go back to your precious computer game and leave me alone!"

"Look, I'm sorry . . ." Sam began.

"Oh, you're sorry? So that makes it all right, does it? Listen, creep, I went out of my way to make you feel welcome, and all you can do is behave like a spoiled brat. I won't make that mistake again. Now, just go away and leave me alone!"

"You're mad at me, aren't you?"

Charly looked at him in astonishment for a moment, then started to laugh.

"Oh my, what a genius!" she eventually managed to get out. "You really are something else!"

Sam was confused now, a condition he usually found himself in at some point when he talked to girls. "Look," he began, "I really am sorry. I didn't mean to hurt your feelings. I was just desperate to get some time to myself. Mom and Dad drive me crazy on these vacations—museums, stately homes, walks in the rain . . . "

"You poor thing!" Charly interrupted sarcastically. "It must be terrible having two parents who take you on vacation and chauffeur you around."

"It's just . . . " Sam found it awkward to explain, "I don't know . . . museums and things give me the creeps. They're so . . . dead."

"What you need," Charly replied, "is a dose of the countryside. Although I don't know why I should go to any trouble for you." She was smiling at him in the way that his mother sometimes did, as though he were some sort of perplexing but mildly amusing puzzle. "Get your jacket and something to eat. I'll show you something that isn't dead."

They followed the path and soon the hedge on their right broadened and became a small patch of woodland, which they entered over a stile. The ground rose steadily, and the path snaked back and forth across the slope, weaving between the trunks of great trees.

"Beech," said Charly unexpectedly, pointing around them. "They like chalky soil, but not much grows under them." Sam saw that she was right—the ground was bare except for a deep brown carpet of beech leaves, lit to copper here and there where a shaft of sunlight broke through the canopy. Traces of the morning's fog lingered among the trees, and sunbeams moved like searchlights across the ground.

"You seem to know a lot about, you know, trees and stuff," said Sam, with grudging respect.

"Granddad taught me," Charly replied. "He used to take me walking. We'd collect blackberries, catch small fish. He knew all the best places to go, all the names of things. We used to walk for miles. And my mom, she's really into herbs and folklore, so I've learned stuff from her, too . . . " She glanced at Sam from the corner of her eye and said, "She's a Wiccan."

"She's from Wigan? I thought you were local." Sam looked puzzled.

"Not Wigan, you idiot! She's a Wiccan. It's, well, no . . . you'll laugh. Everyone does."

Sam was intrigued now. "No I won't. I promise. Go on." Charly looked doubtful.

"Well . . . she's a witch."

"Ah, right. A witch." Sam had to bite the inside of his cheek. "Pointy hat, that kind of thing?"

"I knew you'd laugh. Everyone at school thinks it's hilarious. She hasn't got a pointy hat, or a broomstick, or warts."

"Black cat?" asked Sam hopefully.

"Ginger tom, actually," replied Charly. "She believes in the power of the natural world, the cycles of nature, that kind of stuff." Charly looked uncomfortable, as if this was something she had never become used to explaining. "It doesn't seem weird if you've grown up with it, okay? She's always used herbs and taught me charms and things, as long as I can remember. She doesn't dance around in the nude or sacrifice chickens or anything like that."

"So, you're one of these, these Wiccans, too?" asked Sam rather nervously.

"I'm not as into it as Mom is," replied Charly, "but I know a few things. It's interesting. Don't worry," she smiled, "I'm not going to turn you into a toad or anything, although I probably should. I'm too young to be initiated." Charly seemed relieved that Sam hadn't collapsed in hysterics at her revelation.

As they wandered through the sunlit wood, kicking through the carpet of leaves, Charly explained, "It's kind of like a religion—there are festivals and rituals and a god and goddess—but it's more practical, more down-to-earth. It's pretty much all about nature. The festivals—they're called Sabbats—celebrate the cycle of the year, like the winter solstice on the shortest day, and Lammas, that's a sort of harvest festival at the start of August."

"Sounds, er, interesting," was the best that Sam could manage.

"And the Goddess and the Horned God," continued Charly, "they're the male and female sides of nature. All the goddesses you've ever heard of—Isis, Diana, Aphrodite—are all aspects of the One Goddess."

Sam, who had never heard of any goddesses, tried to look interested but was starting to feel very much out of his depth. "So," he said, clutching at something Charly had mentioned, "what about this Horned God? Is he the devil?"

"No, stupid! Wiccans don't believe in the devil. That's just something that people made up, 'cuz they were scared of witches. There's only really one rule in Wicca. It's called the Rede, and it says, 'An' it harm none, do what thou wilt.'"

"Sorry," sighed Sam, "now you really are talking gibberish."

"It's old-fashioned English. It means, 'As long as you don't hurt anybody, do whatever you like.'"

"Hmmm," Sam was impressed. "Sounds good to me."

They crossed another stile and found themselves on the upper edge of the wood. The sun had burned away the last traces of mist, and the day was turning warm. They emerged from the shadows of the trees into bright sunlight. Sam was finding the climb hard work, but Charly strode up the hillside with ease, and Sam was determined to keep up. After fifteen minutes or so of steady climbing, the path began to level out, and they emerged onto the top of the hill.

"Here we are," announced Charly, "Brenscombe Hill." Sam stopped, trying not to pant, and turned to look.

"Wow!"

The whole of the Isle of Purbeck was laid out in front of him like a rich carpet. The farmhouse was barely visible below them, on the far side of the wood. A faint blue haze of smoke rising from the trees marked its position. Beyond it, the church spire and roofs of Brenscombe village could just be seen in the distance. All around, the patchwork of fields stretched away and was lost to the distance. Looking to his left and right, Sam saw that the hill they stood on was as Charly described, very long and slightly curved but not very wide, as if a huge animal had burrowed just beneath the surface and left this trail behind. His eye followed the curve to the left where he could just see the sparkle of the sea.

"Wow!" he repeated.

"Don't tell me you're impressed, city boy!" remarked Charly with a grin. They sat side by side on the springy turf, and Charly began to point out features in the landscape. "See how the hill curves around, then there's a sort of gap? That's Corfe Castle. It defends the gap into the Isle of Purbeck. You can see the road to Swanage down there and the railroad line—the old steam railroad." Sam nodded, remembering the station in Swanage. "In fact, there's a train over there."

Sam followed her pointing finger and made out a plume of white smoke, although the train and the track were hidden from view.

"Come on," said Charly, jumping to her feet, "let's head this way."

They turned toward the sea and began to walk along the ridge. The turf had been cropped by rabbits and grazing sheep and had a spring to it that made walking a pleasure. It was studded here and there with tiny flowers, and a few blue butterflies tumbled from blossom to blossom.

"This part is Brenscombe Hill," Charly explained, "but farther on, it becomes Nine Barrow Down."

"Barrow? As in wheelbarrow?" Sam asked.

"No, silly. A barrow is an ancient burial mound. Important people were buried in a kind of stone tomb, and the whole thing was covered with soil, to make a long mound."

"Like this hill?" joked Sam.

"Yes." Charly looked thoughtful. "I hadn't thought of it before, but I suppose so."

They continued in silence.

The sun shone down from a deep blue sky, and a clean wind blew up the slope from the country below. Skylarks poured out their song. Sam was surprised to find that he was enjoying himself. He gazed at the fields, lost in thought. Suddenly, he saw a dark shape running across an expanse of green grass, far below.

"What's that?" he asked Charly.

"What?"

He pointed. "Down there, running across that field. Big black thing."

"Just a dog, I suppose," Charly replied, but something about her manner suggested that she was trying to convince herself.

"It doesn't move like a dog. That reminds me, we saw something like this on the way here. Just before we got to Brenscombe, Dad had to brake quickly, and there in the middle of the road was a big black animal that looked like a huge cat. It just kind of stared at us, cool as anything, then walked away. Any ideas?"

"No! No. It was probably just what you said—a big cat."
Charly seemed strangely tense.

"No way," replied Sam, sensing her anxiety, "this thing
was massive. You know something, don't you? Something
you're not telling me."

"It's nothing—just rumors around the village. People
have been seeing things, like big black cats or black pan-
thers, for the last six months or so. And a few sheep have
been found dead, but that could have been dogs. They figure there are two of these things."

"Hmmm, well it seems to have disappeared now," said
Sam. "Let's get going."

They continued along the crest of the ridge, but Charly
was quiet, obviously disturbed by what they had seen.
Clouds had formed, where the breeze from the sea was
forced to rise by the bulk of the hill, and the day was turning cooler. Without the sunshine, the top of the hill felt
bleak and lonely.

Something—maybe the cold breeze—had driven the
skylarks away, and the land seemed empty without their
song. Here and there, round, white pieces of chalk stuck
out of the short turf, like the ends of bones pushing
through the skin of the hill. Sam was starting to feel kind
of odd. Maybe it was the unaccustomed exercise, maybe he
just needed some lunch. He felt light-headed, and his skin
was prickling. He shook his head and hurried after Charly.
Up ahead, he could see a long, low mound.

"Is that one of those barrows?" he asked.

"Yes." Charly's spirits lifted at the sight of the barrow.
"And just behind it, there are a couple of tumuli."

"Ugh! Sounds horrible!" replied Sam.

"No, idiot. Tumuli are like barrows, only smaller and circular. See those two little lumps over there? This is one of my favorite places." She skipped toward the ancient earthworks, Sam trailing behind.

They decided to stop for lunch and sat out of the wind with their backs against the springy grass of the barrow's sloping side. Charly pulled a bottle of lemonade out of her backpack and offered it to Sam. Munching on a sandwich, she explained. "Granddad used to bring me up here, and later, after he died, I came here with Mom. She told me stories about the place. A great king is supposed to be buried in this barrow, a great hero with all his treasure, but nobody's ever been able to get inside. She taught me a rhyme, which sort of goes with the barrow, a traditional thing, I guess, and we used to sing it and dance around the barrow."

Sam looked amused. "A Wiccan thing, huh?"

"No, a fun thing. Remember fun?"

"Okay, okay! What did you used to sing?"

"You'll laugh," replied Charly.

"I'm getting pretty good at not laughing. Go on."

Charly stood up, cleared her throat, and turned to face him. With her arms out from her sides, she recited:

> I am the wind upon the sea
> I am the flood across the plain
> I am the hawk above the cliff
> I am the thorn beneath the rose

She dropped her arms and looked slightly embarrassed. "Kind of silly," she said. "It doesn't even rhyme. Mom said there was more of it, but if I ever knew, I've forgotten. What's wrong?"

Sam had gone white and was staring at her as if he had seen a ghost.

"Weird!" he said, eventually. "I know that. I've heard it before, but I can't have. As soon as you started, every hair on the back of my neck stood up."

He scrambled to his feet. The prickling sensation had increased, and his head was throbbing. "Come on!" he said, and sprinted across the grass.

Charly followed him and found him standing, facing the narrow end of the barrow, arms raised at his sides.

"What was it again?" he shouted.

"Sam, what is it? You're acting really odd. Even odder than usual."

"What was it again?" he repeated. "The rhyme?" Charly looked at him uncertainly and began, "I am the wind upon the sea . . . "

"Yes! I am the wind upon the sea—I don't even know what it means, but I know it!" He cleared his throat.

> I am the wind upon the sea
> I am the flood across the plain
> I am the hawk above the cliff
> I am the thorn beneath the rose

He dropped his arms and stared at the end of the barrow, suddenly wondering what the heck he was doing. At least the feeling of tension in his head had gone. He turned to Charly with an embarrassed grin, but she was pointing past him, back to the barrow.

"Look," she said, in a small voice. Sam turned to look.

A vertical crack had appeared in the middle of the barrow, making the grass look as if it was being ripped apart along a seam.

"Sam, come on! I think we should . . ." but Charly never finished the sentence. Her voice was drowned out as two stone doors inside the barrow were flung wide open to reveal a dark figure silhouetted against a blueish light.

chapter 3

At this point, the sensible thing would have been to run, but somehow they couldn't bring themselves to move. The figure before them raised one arm and pointed to them. In a commanding voice, it said "B̶e̶g̶o̶n̶e̶ f̶r̶o̶m̶ t̶h̶i̶s̶ p̶l̶a̶c̶e̶, f̶o̶u̶l̶ s̶p̶i̶r̶i̶t̶s̶!"

Sam and Charly stared at each other in confusion.

After a moment, Charly said, "Er . . . sorry . . . didn't get that . . . "

"Oh, bother!" exclaimed the stranger. "You people are forever changing languages! How's a fellow supposed to keep up? Ahem!" He cleared his throat. "Begone from this place, foul spirits!" it exclaimed. "Oh, I've quite lost the moment now, haven't I? Bother!"

"Who are you calling foul spirits?" asked Sam, whose initial fear was rapidly turning into curiosity.

"Look, couldn't you just run along? I'm expecting someone."

The person walked toward them. On closer inspection, he turned out to be a grimy man, perhaps in his early forties but appearing older because of his straggly hair and a long, unkempt beard. He was wearing a long, shapeless garment covered with stains and cobwebs.

37

"Who are you?" asked Charly.

"I am Wisdom!" exclaimed the figure, throwing his arms wide.

"Well, you may be Wisdom," replied Charly, "but you've got a spider hanging off your ear."

At that moment, they heard a deep growl from behind them. Charly and Sam spun around and saw two black, feline shapes, one emerging from behind each of the two tumuli.

Sam's stomach clenched with fear. "That's what we saw," he gasped. "On the way here, when Dad had to brake. What are they?"

"I don't know," said Charly, edging backward, "but I really think we should get out of here."

The two huge, black cats were slinking toward them, low to the ground, unblinking green eyes fixed on Sam.

"Ah, they are abroad," said the mysterious stranger from behind them. "Dark times, indeed. Come, children. Inside."

Sam and Charly looked at each other. Normally, Sam would never have considered walking into an ancient tomb with a strange man in rags, but, as the two cats closed in, it suddenly seemed a tempting option. The cats paused, pressed close to the ground, blue highlights glistening on their tense shoulder muscles. One drew back its lips from long, viciously curved canine teeth and growled. The sound seemed to shake the earth beneath Sam's feet, and a foul smell drifted toward him, making him want to gag. The second cat shifted its hind legs slightly and tensed, preparing to spring. Sam made up his mind. "Come on!" he shouted, grabbing Charly by the arm, he ran for the interior of the barrow.

He and Charly rushed after the retreating figure into a narrow passageway with a roof just high enough for them to stand; the stranger had to stoop. There was a grating sound and a hollow boom as the doors slammed shut behind them. Shortly, they emerged into a low-ceilinged chamber. The floor was made of bare earth, with the walls and roof of huge slabs of stone, roughly fitted together without mortar. Pale roots hung down through the cracks in the ceiling, and spiders' webs decorated the walls. A strange blue light, with no discernible source or direction, filled the chamber. In the center was a rectangular stone slab that bore a faint depression in the shape of a human figure.

"So," began Charly, "who are you? And spare us the wisdom speech this time."

"Ah, child," began the stranger, "it is not for you to know who I am. You should not be here. This is wrong, all wrong." He began to pace up and down. "And yet, the sign was given. And they are abroad. Ah, if only he were here to guide me . . . " He seemed to be talking to himself.

"What are those things, anyway?" asked Charly. "Apart from abroad, obviously."

"Evil, child! Aye, evil." The strange man peered at her with wild eyes.

"Oh, good. That's reassuring."

"Er, look," said Sam, "this is all a little bit weird. We should be getting back now. Is there any chance you could let us out, assuming those things have gone?"

"Hmm?" The stranger was lost in thought. "Yes, yes! This is all wrong. I must return to my waiting, and you must go. I will place a charm upon you to protect you from those creatures—that much power I have, at least. Then you must go and forget that this ever came to pass."

He walked with them back to the entrance, where, at the touch of his finger, the great doors opened once more. He turned to them, and, with one hand outstretched, his fingers spread, he began to mutter under his breath.

Sam felt the hairs on the back of his neck bristle again. "There," said the stranger, "they will not harm you, for a short while at least. Now go, and forget!"

He turned and marched back into the depths of the barrow, leaving Sam and Charly on the grass, blinking in the light of the sun. The stone doors slammed shut, leaving no trace of a crack.

"So," Sam turned to Charly, "this is the quiet, restful countryside!"

The journey home passed quickly. At first, they were fearful that the two catlike creatures would reappear, but soon they were lost in debate. First, Charly had to convince Sam that this sort of thing didn't happen all the time in the country, not even to Wiccans. Then their conversation turned to the identity of the mysterious stranger. He didn't seem to fit in with the legend of a great king or hero, unless heroes were typically covered in stains and spiders. At last they parted in the farmyard but agreed to meet up the next day, if possible, to discuss the matter further. From the hedgerow that bounded the farmyard, two pairs of green eyes watched them part.

Sam convinced his parents over dinner that his day had been not only educational and healthy, but also good for the development of his social skills. Although somewhat surprised by this abrupt change of character, they seemed happy enough for him to spend the next day in a similar fashion. He went to bed early, too tired by the fresh air, unaccustomed exercise, and excitement to even play with his computer game.

However, not long after he had fallen asleep, he awoke to the sound of something tapping on his bedroom window. Fearing that the black cats had followed him, he rolled over and pulled the curtains open just enough to peer out. Down in the yard below, the light of the moon revealed Charly, bundled up in coat and scarf, about to throw another pebble at his window. She gestured frantically for him to come down. He opened the window and hissed, "What is it?"

"Come down, quickly!" she called. "It's important!"

He hurriedly pulled on some warm clothes and crept downstairs, avoiding the creaky floorboards near his parents' room. Out in the yard, Charly came running up, her breath steaming in the night air.

"It's him," she gasped. "The man from the barrow! He's here!"

"What do you mean he's here?" asked Sam, who was still half asleep.

"Which word don't you understand? He's here! He just turned up! Come on!"

With that, she ran across the farmyard, leaving Sam to follow her to one of the barns where they had collected eggs. There in the straw, wrapped in some of Charly's spare sweaters, was a miserable figure.

"I can't get any sense out of him," said Charly. "He just keeps saying that it's all wrong and that he can't go back."

The stranger looked at Sam. "It's all wrong!" he wailed.

"See what I mean?" asked Charly. They sat down in the straw. "Look," Charly began, "we'll try to help you, but you've got to give us something to go on."

"I can't go back!" wailed the figure.

"Yes, I think we've got that part," said Charly. "Can you be a little more specific?"

"For a start," Sam chipped in, "how about a name? And don't say Wisdom again."

The stranger looked over at Sam with a penetrating stare. "Think this is funny, do you, child? I am Amergin. I am He Who Waits, and I have been awoken before my time, and now I cannot go back."

"You mean you were asleep in that barrow?" asked Charly.

"Aye, child, for many long years. Now I am awoken and cannot return."

"Have you tried counting sheep?" suggested Sam. Charly gave him a kick on the shin.

"What are you waiting for?" continued Charly.

"Not what, child," replied Amergin, "but whom. I await the coming of a great hero, one who will turn back the darkness at a time of danger. The charm has been spoken, and I am awake, but where is the hero?"

"Well, it was Sam here who spoke the charm," Charly pointed out.

"Yes, yes, child," said Amergin impatiently, "and therein lies the problem. I seek a great hero, a warrior. If only he were here to guide me."

"That's the second time you've said that," interrupted Sam. "Who's he?"

"He, child, is my master, the one who entrusted me with this task. The greatest of our craft—Merlin."

"Wow! Merlin the Magician?" Sam was definitely interested now.

"Magician, boy? He is no simple conjurer. He is the greatest amongst us, most learned of this or any other age, philosopher, alchemist, master of the hidden arts . . . "

"So where is he?" asked Charly.

"Well, there was a problem," Amergin looked embarrassed. "You see . . . there was this woman . . . "

"Ah, they're always trouble!" said Sam. Charly stuck her tongue out.

"Ahem. There was, as I say, a woman. Nimue," continued Amergin. "And it was prophesied that she would ensnare Merlin with her wiles, and they would live together in a cave. Or was it a castle? Or a cottage . . . I forget." Amergin's eyes lost focus and he stared into space for a moment. "Anyway," he shook his head to clear his thoughts, "Nimue placed an enchantment upon Merlin . . . or was that Morgan le Fay? Whichever, Merlin and Nimue departed for the castle—or cave—and Merlin asked that I take his place within the barrow, him being somewhat tied up, so to speak. I was his apprentice, do you see? Aye, picked me himself."

"I bet he did," said Charly, rolling her eyes at Sam. "And

you didn't find it strange that Merlin got to live in a castle with a girl and you got to lie in a cold barrow for hundreds of years?"

"Strange?" asked Amergin. "Nay, I was honored! Said I was his best pupil. Wouldn't entrust it to anyone else. Great honor. But now it's all gone wrong!" He slumped back into despair.

"Well, I don't know what to suggest," sighed Sam. "What does our resident Wiccan say?"

Amergin looked up at Charly. "You are a follower of the Goddess?"

"Er . . . not really me so much," admitted Charly, "more my mother."

"I must speak with this woman," Amergin decided, jumping to his feet.

"Oh, no!" Charly looked doubtful. "She'll go crazy if I turn up with you looking like that, jabbering about Merlin and great heroes and stuff."

"Nonsense! If she is a follower of the Craft of the Wise, we are of the same ilk."

Charly and Sam looked at each other. "Ilk?" asked Sam.

"I dunno," said Charly. "Whatever—it's far too late now. It'll have to wait until morning, and we've got to get you cleaned up before you talk to anybody."

The next morning, with his hair and beard trimmed, the worst of the grime cleaned off, and wearing some of Charly's uncle's old clothes, Amergin looked far more respectable. Under the stained robe and the filth of the centuries, he turned out to be a handsome man in the prime of life and in good physical shape for someone who had been lying on a rock for many centuries. Before Charly would introduce him to her mother, however, she had made Amergin agree to a trial run. They were to take a walk into the village of Brenscombe, so he could get a feel for the age in which he had awoken.

Charly picked a few last wisps of straw from Amergin's clothes, looked him up and down, and pronounced that he would do. Together, the three of them set off on foot, taking the winding farm track to the road, then walking along the road's edge as it wound toward the village.

Back at the cottage, Charly's mother, Megan, bustled around the kitchen, taking crockery from the drainer by the old, square stone sink and placing it neatly away in cupboards. She had something on her mind, and she hummed thoughtfully to herself as she worked, gliding around the room as if she were dancing to her own music.

Charly had been acting strangely the past few days, ever since she'd taken up with that boy from the rental cottage. Charly had been prone to fits of solitude after her father had left. Megan thought this was only natural and gave her daughter the freedom she needed, letting her wander onto Brenscombe Hill when the mood took her, knowing that she would return when she was ready. But this latest behavior was something different.

Megan had an eye for human behavior and sometimes could see, when conditions were right, a faint aura around people, a glow of light that told her a lot about how they were feeling. Charly's aura was full of suppressed excitement and the slightest tinge of fear. Something was clearly going on.

Having put away the last of the dishes, Megan paused, deciding that everything was to her liking. She took a key from a hook on the wall and left by the back door.

Crossing her small herb garden, Megan let herself into a low building that was tacked onto the rest of the cottage almost as an afterthought. She flicked the light switch just inside the door and took an apron from its peg on the wall. The room was clearly a workshop, an untidy collection of benches and shelves, cluttered with a bewildering array of pots, cups, vases, and plates, some of them glazed and painted, some with the silky sheen of fresh clay.

When Megan had something on her mind, something she needed to ponder, she liked to work. With her hands occupied, her mind was free to figure out problems. Knotting the apron expertly behind her back, Megan settled into her seat at a potter's wheel in the center of the room. Then, instead of starting work, she paused, eyes closed and head bowed. After a moment, she raised her head and said, "Hail, golden Brighid,"—she pronounced it 'Breed'—"inspirer of us all,"

> Mother of healing, mistress of the arts,
> Lady of every skill—on thee I call
> To pour thy magic into human hearts.
> Bestow thy blessing on the poet's pen,
> The craftsman's chisel, and the healer's hand;
> And guide the work of women and men
> To bring thy beauty into this our land.

With that, she took a lump of wet clay from a bin by her side and smacked it firmly into the center of the spinning wheel.

chapter 4

Sam, Charly, and Amergin arrived in Brenscombe without too much incident, except when a car had passed them, and Amergin had leaped into the hedge. They removed the twigs from his hair and explained about some of the machines he might see.

"And this box," Amergin was saying as they reached the houses that marked the beginning of the main street, "it shows images from all the globe?"

"Yes," explained Sam, "television, lots of moving pictures from all over the world. They're mostly repeats, though."

"Marvellous, marvellous!" said Amergin, stepping out into the main street in front of a car. Charly pulled him back to the curb by the back of his baggy tweed jacket.

"And this gentleman," Amergin thrust one grubby index finger in the direction of a man in a suit. "Why does he talk to himself? Possessed by devils, perchance?"

"Yes," Charly smiled. "Well, no, not really. That thing he's holding to his ear? It's a cell phone. He can talk to people far away."

As he passed, they heard the man saying " . . . yeah, yeah, I'm in a little village. Yeah! Amazing!"

"Ah, what knowledge could be shared, what a meeting of great minds could be achieved with such an engine!" exclaimed Amergin.

"Er, yes, something like that," Charly replied uncertainly.

They paused outside a drugstore. Charly suggested, "Why don't you go in and buy something? We'll give you some money, and you can go in and ask." Amergin looked doubtful. "They get all kinds of strange people in there, tourists and such," she risked a glance at Sam. "They won't notice anything unusual."

Amergin was eventually persuaded to enter the shop, mainly by Charly opening the door and Sam pushing him hard in the small of the back. He stumbled to a halt, looking back wildly at the door before straightening his jacket and walking to the counter. "Hrrrmph. Good day, good wife!" he exclaimed. "I wish to purchase . . . " The girl behind the counter smiled indulgently at him as he looked around the shop. The outlandish name had slipped his memory. He went slightly pink around the ears. "I wish to purchase . . . oh, confound it!"

"It's all right, dear," said the girl, "no need to be shy. I think I can guess what you want."

Several minutes later, Amergin emerged looking triumphant.

"Well, how did it go?" asked Sam.

"There was some confusion; the young lady tried to sell me a small box of some kind, but then I recalled the object of my quest. Behold—mouthwash!" With a flourish, Amergin extracted a green bottle from his jacket.

"Good job," said Charly. "Now, nothing personal, but have a swig and spit it out in the gutter here."

Amergin took a long pull from the bottle, turned bright red, and ejected the mouthwash in a fine, peppermint-flavored spray that drifted off down the street. "Poisoned!" he croaked, with watering eyes.

"Oh, please!" sighed Charly.

They continued along the main street, Amergin craning his neck in every direction to take in the sights. He reminded Sam of a puppy on its first walk, scampering here and there, peering, sniffing. He seemed to find a woman in a telephone booth particularly interesting and had to be dragged away by Charly, leaving a fading patch of foggy breath on the glass and a very puzzled occupant.

Halfway along the street, a small airplane passed overhead, its single engine droning in the clear air. Amergin froze for a moment, staring skyward, and then screamed. "Dragon!" he wailed, clamping his hands over his head and running back and forth.

Seeing nowhere to hide, he darted between two parked cars and into the road, bringing the traffic to a screeching halt. Pausing for a moment and looking wildly around, he jumped onto the nearest hood and trotted nimbly from one car to the next. The hood of the second car made a disturbing clunk as he dropped down onto the far sidewalk, leaving a big dent. Angry drivers were waving their fists, as Sam and Charly picked their way through the chaos after the fleeing wizard.

"Sorry!" shouted Charly to the gaping drivers and astonished passersby. "He's foreign!"

They caught up with Amergin as he crouched, shivering, in a shop doorway, hands still over his head.

"Come on," said Charly sympathetically, "I think you need a cup of tea."

They led Amergin, shooting nervous glances at the sky, into the nearest tea shop. "This will be good, anyway," added Charly. "You can listen to people talking, get the hang of how they speak."

They took a seat at a table in the corner, as close to the other customers as possible. Charly ordered tea and scones from the waitress and nodded at Amergin, directing his attention to the two ladies at the nearest table.

" . . . anyway," said the first lady, sipping daintily at her tea, "I told her, I said, 'There's no need to go taking that tone,' I said, 'not with me,' I said. 'I don't know what you mean,' she said, but she knew, all right. She's always put on airs and graces, that one, ever since they put in the conservatory. Thinks just because they had two weeks in a villa in Málaga, they're better than us."

"Oooh, I know!" replied the second lady.

Charly looked at Sam and raised her eyes to the ceiling. Sam gestured to another table, where a young man was in deep discussion with his girlfriend. Charly tapped Amergin's arm and discreetly pointed in the direction of the couple.

" . . . so," the young man was saying, "if you stick to the same numbers every week, right, you get better odds, right? An' there's some numbers come up more than others, right? Like forty-four, that's a good 'un, always comes up, does forty-four. And thirty-six, that's a good 'un, too. I 'ave one row I pick meself, birthdays and such, and one Lucky Dip. That's the best way."

"And 'ave you won anythin'?" asked the girl.

"Well, once . . . "

Charly sighed. "Well," she said, "perhaps you'd better listen to Sam and me instead."

Just then, the tea arrived: a stainless steel pot, three white china cups, and a plate of thick, golden scones with jam and clotted cream. Sam poured the tea and placed a cup in front of Amergin.

"What is it, child?" asked the wizard, peering suspiciously at the brown liquid. The mouthwash was still fresh in his memory.

"It's just tea," said Sam. "It's made from, well, dried-up leaves, in hot water."

"You should go into advertising," smiled Charly. "You make it sound so-ooo tasty!"

Amergin was still doubtful but picked up the cup daintily between thumb and forefinger and took the most enormous slurp. All around the tearoom, heads turned in their direction.

"Perhaps a little bit quieter?" suggested Sam.

"This is good!" declared the wizard in a loud voice and sucked another mouthful from the surface of the tea, with a noise like a bathtub emptying.

Ignoring the stares of the other customers, Charly showed Amergin how to cut the scones and slather them in thick layers of jam and cream. Picking up his first half-scone, Amergin rammed most of it in his mouth, chewed a couple of times, and said, "Delicious!"

Crumbs sprayed all over the tablecloth, and a significant proportion of the jam and cream hung from his beard and moustache.

"I think you'd better use a napkin," suggested Charly, "or even better, tuck the tablecloth into your belt."

With the tablecloth securely tucked into the front of his trousers, Amergin stuffed the remains of the first scone into his mouth and sat there contentedly, a steady rain of crumbs and clots of cream falling from his mouth.

Just then, the door of the tearoom opened with a jangle of bells, and a girl walked in. She was dressed in black, a leather jacket over a miniskirt and motorcycle boots. Her ears were pierced, not only through the lobes but all around the edges, as were her nose and one eyebrow, and her hair was bright pink.

Amergin leaped to his feet and took a step back. The tablecloth, still tucked into his trousers, came with him, and the tea service clattered to the floor. Cups shattered, and tea washed across the clean tiles.

Amergin flung one hand in the direction of the girl, finger pointing rigidly, and cried, "Begone, foul demon!" in a positive fountain of scone crumbs.

"What's your problem!" replied the girl, looking alarmed.

"Hie thee back to thy dark abode!" bellowed Amergin. "Come, children!" With that, he took Sam and Charly by the arms and dragged them out of the tearoom, the tablecloth trailing behind him, ignoring the cries of protest from the waitress.

"Amergin! Amergin!" shouted Charly, "Slow down!"

She and Sam managed to calm the wizard and directed him to a nearby bench. Settling down next to him, Charly said, "All right. We need to explain a few things. Now, where do I start . . . ?"

An hour later, having smoothed things over with the tearoom waitress, Charly and Sam reviewed the situation. They agreed that Amergin was making sufficient progress that he might be able to speak to Charly's mother without appearing too odd. However, they had yet to come up with a plausible explanation of who he was and why he was following them around. They were still debating this problem as they headed out of town when, at the top of the main street opposite the church, Amergin suddenly brought them both to a halt by grabbing the backs of their coats. "Stay!" he hissed.

"We're not sheepdogs," protested Sam.

"What is it?" asked Charly, sensing the tension in Amergin.

"Yonder, by the church gate." He nodded across the street. Following his gaze, Charly noticed two tall figures, dressed in black suits and wearing black sunglasses.

"Wow," exclaimed Sam, "it's the Men in Black!"

"His agents," murmured Amergin. "His power grows."

At that moment, the two men seemed to notice them. They exchanged glances and started across the street toward them. "Quickly! We must flee! I cannot resist them yet." Amergin pulled them into motion and broke into a run toward the center of the village. Behind them, the two dark figures set off in pursuit, running with surprising speed. The gap quickly narrowed.

Ahead, Sam noticed that a bus had pulled up at the curb, and the last of the waiting passengers had just boarded. "Charly!" he shouted. "The bus!"

After a moment's confusion, Charly realized what he meant. Grabbing Amergin by his baggy jacket, she yelled at him, "Quick! On here!" Amergin looked doubtful but allowed himself to be bundled onto the waiting bus. Charly and Sam clattered up the steps close on his heels, Charly rummaging in her pocket for change. Moving down the central aisle with their tickets, Charly saw that Amergin was clinging tightly to an upright metal handrail, eyes screwed shut. "Amergin," she said softly. "Amergin! You can sit down." She gestured to one of the empty seats.

Amergin opened one eye a fraction and, with a sickly grin, sank heavily into a window seat.

As the doors closed and the bus began to pick up speed, Sam saw two dark figures pounding alongside. Their speed was incredible; they were nearly ahead of the bus as it picked its way along the narrow street. It seemed likely that they'd reach the next bus stop in time to flag down the bus and board. Then, one of the two men collided with a startled pedestrian and spun off into a revolving rack of postcards, his momentum lost. The second figure came to a halt by the side of the first, whose sunglasses had fallen off in the collision. As the bus passed them, Sam and Charly had a brief view of his face. His features were unremarkable, except for one thing: he glared back at them through bright green eyes.

chapter 5

"Okay," said Charly as the bus left the village and they had recovered their breath. "I think it's about time you told us what's going on."

"I have told you of my task, that I was charged to await the coming of a great hero, to act as his guide and mentor, and that I was awakened before my time. You need know no more." Amergin had slumped in his seat and was staring out of the window at the passing fields.

"Oh, no," joined in Sam. "If we're going to get chased around by aliens, then I think we have a right to know why."

"Yes," agreed Charly, "this obviously involves us in some way. You owe us some kind of explanation."

Amergin sighed. "Very well. But where to begin?"

Sam had no shortage of questions. "Several times now you've mentioned he and him. Like, 'His power has grown!'" Sam did a creditable impression of Amergin. "So, who's he?"

"As good a place to start as any. Child," Amergin faced Sam, "what know you of good and evil?"

"Well," Sam began, "I know that there are things you shouldn't do, like lying and stealing . . . "

"No, no, no, child. You speak of morals, of the rules that humans make so they may live together in peace. I ask what know you of absolute good and absolute evil?"

Sam looked a little nervous, like when a teacher asked him a particularly difficult question in class. "Errrr . . ." he began.

"Consider then, child, the light," Amergin began. "At night, we see the stars, but in the daytime they are hidden from us. The light of the sun masks them. We need the dark in order to perceive the light of the stars. Yes?"

Sam and Charly nodded.

"And in a deeper sense, there cannot be light unless there is darkness in which it may exist. Imagine, then, that the same is true for good and evil. Look around us." He gestured out of the bus window, at the rolling landscape of fields and hedges. Cloud shadows were tracking across the bulk of the Purbeck Hills to their left, and a beam of sunlight briefly illuminated the ruin of Corfe Castle rising in front of them.

"There is much that is good and fair in the world. Of itself, whether you and I are here to witness it, the land is beautiful. But that good cannot exist unless there is evil against which to judge it. Just as there cannot be light without the dark."

He fell silent. Sam and Charly looked at each other. "Evil exists in this land, as surely as you and I exist. It works its wickedness through the hearts of people, but it has two chief servants—the Dhouls—you saw them just now in human form and before, at the barrow, in the shape of great beasts."

"The big cats?" exclaimed Charly in surprise. "Those two men were the big black cats?"

"You saw their eyes. Such creatures can take many forms, but their eyes cannot be hidden. They are gruagach, people of power who were ensnared by the evil of which I spoke."

"Does he, this evil, I mean," asked Sam, "does he have a name?"

"He has had many names down the ages—you will have heard some of them—but to the wise he is known simply as the Malifex."

"And this . . . Malifex?" asked Charly. "What does he want?"

"What he has always wanted, child," replied the wizard gravely. "To shift the balance from light to dark, from life to death. He will not rest until all goodness and beauty are lost from the land and until the greed and envy in the hearts of people have despoiled the world."

"But . . . why?" protested Sam. "Why would he want to do that?"

"Why? Why does fire consume? Why does the sea forever erode the land? It is his nature; he is evil, destruction, death. He has his place in the Wheel of Life, as do birth, creation, light. But the two sides should be in balance. The Malifex seeks always to shift the balance."

The three of them fell silent.

"So," Charly asked after several minutes had passed, "where do you fit into all this?"

"As I have told," Amergin replied, "the great Merlin set me to wait against a time when I would be needed. Good and evil have waged war in this land down the ages; first one winning the upper hand, then the other. In times of peace, people forget the face of darkness, forget the battles, and slowly the evil rises again. When last the dark tide was turned back, the wise made provision against the future—I was charged to wait, so that the great hero who would lead the next battle could benefit from the experience of the past. I am the bridge between past and present."

The bus had taken them past the foot of Corfe Castle and had turned east. They were now traveling along the northern side of Brenscombe Hill, heading for the village of Studland.

"We'd better decide where to get off," suggested Sam. "We ought to be getting back."

"Yes, you're right," Charly agreed. "If we get off somewhere along this road, we can go up over the hill, past Amergin's barrow, and drop down to the farm the way we walked yesterday."

Charly got up and walked to the front of the bus and spoke briefly to the driver. When she returned, she announced, "There's a bus stop halfway along this road, near a farm. He'll drop us off there."

A few minutes later, the bus pulled to a halt, and the driver beckoned for them to get off. Standing at the side of the road in a cloud of diesel fumes, Charly pointed, "This way!"

Not far along the road, back the way they had come, was an area of woodland toward which Charly led them. Soon the trees closed in on both sides, overhanging the road and cutting out the light. Before entering this tunnel of trees, Sam paused. Maybe it was the gloom ahead, but suddenly he felt uneasy. He glanced to his left, to the slope of Brenscombe Hill rising above them. In the distance on the hillside, but growing rapidly larger, he could see two dark, feline shapes in full flight.

"Quickly!" he cried. "They're coming!" and broke into a run.

The three of them pounded along the road until Amergin shouted, "This way! It may still be here!" and veered off the road into the trees. Charly followed, but Sam felt compelled to stop and look behind him. In the patch of light where the trees arched over the road, two squat figures were silhouetted. Sam thought he could see four points of emerald light.

Coming to his senses, he dived off into the trees after Charly and Amergin, but by now they were lost from sight. Sam ran in the direction they had been heading, angling away from the road, but was forced to dodge around trees and tangles of brambles and soon lost his bearings. After a few minutes of thrashing through the undergrowth, he stopped and listened for a sign of the others.

Suddenly, he heard a scream to his left, which could only be Charly. With a terrible feeling of dread, he plunged off in the direction of the sound. The undergrowth became more densely tangled, but in his panic he dragged himself through the smallest gaps and was scraped by thorns and lashed by overhanging branches. All of a sudden, he stumbled free and found himself at the edge of a small clearing.

In an instant he took in the scene: daylight streamed

through the trees to reveal a circle of standing stones, tall and lichen-encrusted, partly choked with dead grass. Charly stood between two of the stones, staring forward in horror. Amergin stood in the center of the circle and around him prowled the two black cats, bodies low to the ground and muscles tensed, ready to pounce.

All this registered on Sam in a flash. He felt the hairs on the back of his neck begin to prickle, as they had outside the barrow, and a feeling of tension began to pound in his head. With a wordless cry, he leaped forward into the circle, past a surprised Charly, and came to a halt between the two cats. Two pairs of emerald eyes turned to focus on him.

chapter 6

With one hand pointing toward each of the cats, fingers spread, Sam screamed, "Get away from him!" There was a soundless flash of light that flung him backward onto the grass. The circle of stones seemed to swirl around him and collapse inward. Everything went black.

Some time later, Sam came to his senses. His head was in Charly's lap, and Amergin was bending over him, peering into his eyes.

"Have they gone?" asked Sam, shakily.

"Aye, lad. They are gone . . . for now," replied Amergin gently.

"What . . . ?" Sam began. "What happened? What made them go?"

"You made them go, child. It was you." Amergin looked at him with a strange mixture of admiration and sadness.

"Me? How?"

"Ah, my friend, how indeed? There is only one explanation that fits the facts: that everything I have feared is true, and our doom is come."

"I don't get it," Sam said, sitting up. "What have you feared? What facts?"

Amergin sat back in the center of the circle, his fingers

steepled together. The sun was low in the sky and had dropped below the encircling treetops, plunging the clearing into premature twilight.

"Consider," began Amergin, "that I was tasked by the wisest of the age to await the coming of a great hero, one who would turn back the tide of darkness. The great Merlin himself cast the spell that plunged me into my long slumber. Do you think it likely that he would have allowed me to be awoken before the time was right? Consider also, that I find myself in a world where the Craft is all but lost, where the old ways are utterly forgotten. Except . . . except that the one who woke me from my sleep," he turned back to Sam, "displays all the signs of a great power. For only such power could have turned aside those evil creatures from their purpose. So what else can I conclude?" He looked from one to the other.

"Nope . . . sorry," said Sam, "you're not making any sense."

"It is you, child! You woke me from sleep! You have power over the creatures of the Malifex—you are the hero I seek!"

"Oh, come on!" interrupted Charly. "No offense, Sam," she glanced at him before turning back to Amergin, "but he's not hero material, believe me. He's a city kid. He didn't even know where eggs come from. He plays computer games!"

"No offense, huh?" Sam glared at her. "But she's right." He stood and looked down at Amergin. "I'm not a hero. I'm just here on vacation, and if I don't get back soon, my parents are going to start worrying. I know there's something weird going on here, but you're going to have to figure it out yourself. Good luck. I hope you find your hero." He turned and stalked off through the trees.

"We're going to have to go after him, you know," Charly said, scrambling to her feet. "He's got no idea where he's going, for one thing."

She turned and set off after Sam. A moment later, she heard Amergin shout, "Child! Help me!" She turned back.

"I've got a name, you know," she said, rather crossly. "What do you want?"

"You will have to help me, chil . . . er . . . Charly. I can't get up." Amergin looked embarrassed.

"Why not? Are you hurt?" Charly was suddenly concerned. She had forgotten Amergin's close shave with the Dhouls.

"No, not hurt exactly. Oh, confound it! Look, I've been lying on a slab of rock for a considerable length of time. I can't sit cross-legged as well as I used to. Give me your hand." Charly reached down and hauled him to his feet, where he proceeded to hobble around rubbing his knee. "Ah, child," he said with a sigh. "I have much work ahead of me, and I feel my age. What is it?"

"Charly. My name's Charly!" She stamped off in the direction that Sam had taken.

"Ah, Merlin," muttered Amergin, going after her. "You never mentioned this part."

They caught up with Sam, who allowed himself to be guided to the footpath that took them over Brenscombe Hill toward home. He had, in fact, been heading in entirely the wrong direction and was in a foul mood.

There was little conversation on the way back. It was late afternoon by the time they reached the cluster of farm buildings. In the farmyard, they came to an awkward halt. After a moment, Sam said, "Look, I think I'd better spend some time with my parents. They'll be getting suspicious. I'll ... I'll see you around." He turned and walked off in the direction of the cottage.

"Well," Charly turned to Amergin, "I'd better get you bedded down in the barn for the night. I'll bring out some food to you later. And tomorrow, I think it's time you met my mother."

The next morning, armed with a few more of her uncle's castoff clothes and a story she had been working on all night, Charly went to find Amergin. She found him in one of the less frequently used barns, still asleep in a pile of hay. After dressing him in the most presentable clothes, she began to brief him on the cover story she had invented.

"Okay," she said, plucking a few final strands of straw from his hair, "have you got all that?"

"I think so," replied Amergin uncertainly.

"Good, stay calm. Skip the thees and thous and try not to talk too much. I'll cover for you if you look like you're blowing it."

They made their way around to the cottage Charly shared with her mother. Opening the door, Charly shouted "Mom! Visitor!" After a moment, a woman in a plastic apron appeared in the hallway. Her hair, spilling out of a collection of barrettes and clips, was the same shade of auburn as Charly's and hung in wisps around her face. Her glasses were perched on the end of her nose and were in grave danger of falling off at any moment. Her hands, which she held up at shoulder height with the palms toward her, were covered in a wet, gray substance.

"Honey, I was just in the middle of throwing. Oh, hello!" Charly's mom smiled vaguely over her glasses. "I'm Megan. I won't shake hands." She grimaced and wiggled her fingers.

Amergin threw his arms out to the sides and began, "I am Wisdom!" Charly kicked him sharply in the leg.

"This is Mr. Wisdom, Mom!" she interrupted. "Er, Norman . . . Wisdom." She winced to herself. "He's . . . er . . . a historian. He's on vacation—we met him in the village yesterday. He wanted to talk to someone about local legends, folk customs, that sort of thing."

"I see," said her mother uncertainly. "Well, I'm in the middle of throwing a pot—I'm a potter, you see," she wiggled her fingers again at Amergin, "—but if Charly could put on the tea kettle, I'll only be a few minutes. Then we can talk."

Two hours and several cups of tea later, Amergin and Megan were still deep in conversation. Although many centuries separated them, they shared a common core of experience, and each was able to fill gaps in the other's knowledge. Blank spaces began to appear on the bookshelves as Charly scurried back and forth with titles such as *Chalk Hill-figures*, *Stone Circles of Britain*, *Sacred Dorset*, *Eight Sabbats for Witches*, and *The Old Straight Track*. The hands of the clock crept toward midday, and Charly was sent off to the kitchen for sandwiches. The rest of the time she spent curled in a comfy armchair in the corner of the study, listening to the flow of discussion between the two grown-ups.

By the middle of the afternoon, they had begun to slow down. Eventually the three of them found themselves sitting in a companionable silence, nursing empty tea mugs.

"Well," said Charly's mom, "I hope that's answered all your questions, although you seem to know far more about things than I do. I really ought to be getting back . . . " She smiled apologetically at Amergin. "Are you staying somewhere locally, Mr. Wisdom?"

"Err . . . I haven't really . . . " Amergin began.

"Mr. Wisdom said earlier that he was still looking for somewhere to stay," Charly explained hurriedly.

"That's odd. I was sure Charly said you were staying somewhere in the area."

"Hoping to, dear lady. I have not yet found permanent lodgings."

"Well," Charly's mom looked thoughtful. "I suppose if you are struggling, there's always the guest room . . . " She glanced at Charly.

"I could go and clear out some of the junk, I suppose." Charly tried not to look triumphant.

"How would that suit you, Mr. Wisdom?"

"Dear lady, I would be indebted to you." The look on Amergin's face suggested that he was anticipating sleeping on something other than a slab of rock or a pile of straw for the first time in a very long time.

"You'll need to get your belongings presumably?"

"Er, yes. Yes. Of course." Amergin looked sheepish.

"I'll give Mr. Wisdom a hand with his things, Mom," volunteered Charly and led him out into the farmyard. Once outside, she crowed, "Yes! Result! All we need to do is hang out here for a while, then I'll sneak you back in. Mom'll never notice that you haven't got any luggage. I'll try and get you some more clothes, a toothbrush, that kind of stuff. What's the matter?"

Amergin had a strange look on his face. "Ah, I am far from my own time, my friend, far from the people I left behind. I had not realized how that would feel. I am grateful for your kindness. Grateful to you and to your mother." He looked, suddenly, very ordinary and kind of tired.

Charly gave him a sympathetic smile. "How did you end up, you know, here? Why you?"

"Why me? I have asked myself the same question a thousand times. It is a long tale."

"Well," said Charly, "we've got plenty of time." They had wandered through the outbuildings and emerged in the old orchard. The day had turned fine and warm; dappled sunlight danced under their feet. Amergin sat on the grass with his back against a gnarled old apple tree. He gestured for Charly to sit in front of him.

"Many years ago, more years than I care to remember, I was a bard. You know what a bard is?"

Charly nodded. "Like a poet?"

"Yes, a poet and a musician. Such was my prowess that I became a chieftain among my tribe, the Milesians, for such skills as I had were honored in that time. Under the leadership of the sons of Míl, we left Spain in threescore and five ships and sailed to the land you know as Ireland.

After many battles, we took the land for our own. I settled with my people at Inber Mor, and we were content. I grew in skill as I practiced down the years, until, at the height of my powers, I wrote a song."

He fell silent, gazing into the distance with a sad smile on his lips. The only sound to be heard was the drone of insects in the grass. "Ahhh, it was such a song! Everything I knew, everything I had learned, all the love I had for my land and my people, I put into that song. And something happened." He glanced at Charly before continuing.

"Later, they told me that, through the power of my song, I had opened a window into the whole of creation. I'm sure they are right; I do not know. All I knew was that, for a time that seemed like eternity but which was, in fact, less than a day, I felt connected to all things. I could see all things. No, I was all things, past and future. And for a long time after that I was not as other men. I had power over beasts, I spoke the languages of the birds, the seasons moved to my command, but I had no training, no discipline. I had become what the wise called a wild talent. I grew reckless with my power, and my people began to fear me. But I cared not; for they grew old and died, and I did not. I ran in the hills with the deer, flew as an eagle, became a myth, a spirit that haunted the wild places. It was there that Merlin came to me and took me as his apprentice."

He leveled his gaze at Charly. "If it were not for him, perhaps I would be a myth still. So when he asked me if I would take his place in the barrow, what other answer should I have given?"

Charly was silent for a while, then she asked, "You said you became all things, past and future—does that mean you have seen the future?"

"Not in the way you mean," said Amergin ruefully. "I have seen the shape of the future, like an eagle sees a city. It sees an outline, the city walls, the pattern of streets but could say nothing of the lives of the people in their individual homes. I remember the whole of time, if I remember it at all, as a shape, a taste, a feeling, nothing more. I could not have said that you and I would be sitting here, now, talking as we are."

"And this song of yours," asked Charly, "how did it go?"

"Ah, that is an easier question. Part of it you know—it was the charm that awoke me from my slumber."

"That old thing?" Charly exclaimed. "Mom taught me that when I was a kid!"

"It is flattering that it is still remembered, although there was more, much more."

"Go on, then," Charly prompted.

"Let me see . . . " Amergin stared into space, then began:

I am the hills where poets walk
I am the lure from beyond world's end
I am the spear that rears for blood
I am the tear the sun lets fall . . .

His voice trailed off, lost in the memories of the past. Charly broke the silence. "Well, it's very, er, nice. And you say it opened a window into creation?"

Amergin snapped back to the present, looking rather defensive. "Well, it was the tune, as well. It had a very catchy tune, people were humming it for months, very popular. If I had a lute, I'd . . . anyway," he sniffed, "you had to be there."

"Hmmm," Charly sounded unconvinced. "So, do you have any idea how long you were, you know, asleep?"

"Ah, I have given the question much consideration, my friend. Much of the history of my people seems to be forgotten, but from what I have gleaned in your mother's books, I was born some three hundred years before this, this Jesus Christ."

"Three hundred B.C.!" exclaimed Charly. "That means you're . . . two thousand, three hundred years old!"

"Yes," agreed Amergin with a note of pride, "that is rather impressive, is it not?"

"And what will happen to you now?"

"Hmmm?"

"I mean will you, well, live forever or, or suddenly get really old and wrinkly and crumble into dust or something?"

Amergin gave her a stern look. "You have some strange ideas, young lady. I have aged, though very slowly, during my long sleep. Now, I believe, time will run its natural course, and I will grow old like any other mortal."

"Good," replied Charly. "So you'll be around for a while yet."

"Oh, yes," Amergin smiled. "I will be around for a while."

Sam, badly troubled by the events of the previous day, was awoken early by the daily chorus of the cattle on their way to be milked. His parents thought he seemed subdued over breakfast, but they put it down to being tired after the previous day's exercise. Their destination for the day was Corfe Castle, which Sam had passed with Charly and Amergin on the bus the day before.

He had paid little attention at the time and, as the car pulled into the village, was surprised by the size of the castle. The ridge, of which Brenscombe Hill was a part, was interrupted here by an abrupt gap, as if some great prehistoric cataclysm had broken its back. In the gap was a conical mound, the road winding around its foot, and on top of this mound stood the ruins of Corfe Castle, perfectly placed to defend the entrance to the Isle of Purbeck. Time, however, had taken its toll on the castle. The central keep was reduced to a broken shell, with one column of intact stonework separated from the rest of the structure and rising like a warning finger above the village. From the keep, ruined walls, punctuated by round towers and fragments of other buildings, snaked down the slopes of the mound.

Sam's father paid their entrance fee, and they made their way up the track toward the castle. Sam didn't really mind visiting places like this. They were less stifling than museums. He discovered, with a kind of morbid glee, that the history of the castle was peppered with tales of siege, war, and betrayal. Sam left his parents poring over a guidebook and wandered through the ruins, his imagination restoring the walls and buildings, peopling them with soldiers, peasants, knights, and their horses.

Pausing in his explorations, Sam noticed idly that his parents had struck up a conversation with another visitor, a tall man in a dark suit. As Sam peered down at them from the wall where he stood, the man turned to look at

71

him as if he had sensed Sam's gaze. Sam felt somehow uneasy at this and decided to join his parents.

"This is our son, Sam," explained his father as he came to stand with them, then continued chatting to the dark stranger about local tourist attractions. Sam examined the man curiously. He was tall, well built, and had the look of a successful businessman. It was difficult to guess his age. His hair, greased back from a high forehead, was jet black, but he seemed to be in his late forties, with a maze of tiny lines at the corners of his eyes and two sharp creases running from his nose down either side of his mouth. This gave his mouth a downturned look, as if he was troubled by a lingering bad taste.

As his parents and the stranger spoke, Sam became aware of a strange phenomenon. Although the conversation continued uninterrupted, he noticed that the stranger was staring at him. He glanced at his parents, but they seemed oblivious, talking on and on as if they had the man's full attention. He began to feel scared. Suddenly, he heard, or perhaps felt, a deep voice with no obvious source or direction.

"They would not hear you if you cried out, child," said the voice. "You and I have, shall we say, stepped out of their time for a moment."

Sam realized that the voice was somehow coming from the dark stranger. He looked around wildly at his parents, but they continued their conversation, nodding in response to words Sam could not hear.

"You cannot succeed, you do realize that?" asked the voice.

"I don't understand," stuttered Sam. "Who are you?"

"Don't play the innocent with me, child. You may think that Amergin has explained all to you, but he is a fool. He is far from his own time and knows not how my power has grown. I have succeeded far beyond the worst fears of Merlin and his lackeys. Understand this—there is no hope. Forget your petty victory over my servants yesterday. Forget your quest and the lies of that fool Amergin and go home."

"You're him, aren't you?" said Sam, staring in horror. "The one Amergin was talking about? The Malifex?"

The voice chuckled. "Maker of Evil . . . yes, that name has been given to me. Not one I would perhaps choose for myself. In this media age, I realize how important image is. I go by other names now. Hearken to me, child—abandon your quest and depart. We wouldn't want anything . . . unfortunate to happen to you, or your parents now, would we?" He raised one arched black eyebrow and smiled an unpleasant smile.

Turning away from Sam, the Malifex slipped back into the flow of the conversation. Sam's father was saying, " . . . to have met you. Drop by sometime. Like I said, we're here for the rest of the week."

"Most kind," replied the stranger, "I may well do that." He turned to smile at Sam once more before bidding them all good day and striding off toward the castle exit.

"Who was that, Dad?" asked Sam, trying to keep the fear from his voice.

"A fellow called Mr. Halifax, something big in government civil service. Has a cottage not far from here. Very knowledgable about the local area, particularly its history." Sam's father looked impressed. "I invited him to drop by the cottage one evening. What's the matter?"

Sam looked pale. "Nothing. He just . . . he just gave me the creeps."

"Sam," admonished his mother, "that's not nice. Anyway, you don't have to be there. You could go and see Charly." Sam wasn't sure which option he liked least.

After they had explored the castle to his father's satisfaction, Sam and his parents had a quick walk around the village. For a horrible moment, Sam thought they would have to go to the model village, where all of Corfe and its castle were reproduced in miniature, but his parents were getting hungry.

After lunch in one of the tearooms, they set off for Wareham, an attractive small town a few miles to the north. There they strolled up and down the main street and ate ice cream cones beside the Frome River, where swans were mirrored in the smooth-flowing water. Much against his will, Sam was dragged into a small museum devoted to Lawrence of Arabia, who had once lived in the area and whose statue stood in the nearby church. Then, after stopping at a small supermarket to buy food, they headed back to the cottage.

His mother was preparing dinner when Sam, up in his room with his computer game, heard a knock at the door. A few moments later, his mother called his name, and he ran downstairs, fearing that Mr. Halifax had come already.

"Sam, it's your friend, Charly."

"Mom!" hissed Sam, "I don't want to see her!"

But the door was open, and Charly was standing there. His mother scowled at him and gestured toward the door, so Sam had little choice but to go. Once they were outside, Sam said, "Look, I don't want to see you. I can't see you, okay?" He glanced nervously around the farmyard. If the Malifex caught him talking to Amergin . . .

"Oh, don't be so silly!" exclaimed Charly. "We've got news. Come on."

With that, she turned and set off across the yard. Sam hesitated for a moment, glanced around once more and then ran after her. Striding toward Charly across the farmyard was an unfamiliar figure, aristocratic in a tweed jacket and corduroy trousers, with a swept-back mane of dark hair. As he got closer, Sam realized it was Amergin, freshly showered and clean shaven. "What progress humankind has made!" he exclaimed as Sam and Charly drew near. "The shower, the razor, the shampoo! Good day, my friend!" he called to Sam.

Charly turned to Sam. "Amergin's been having a great time with my mother. She's letting him stay in our guest room, and they spend all their time with their noses buried in old books. Amergin is posing as a vacationing historian. His name's Mr. Wisdom." She paused. "Er . . . Norman Wisdom."

Sam raised an eyebrow at her.

"I was thinking on my feet, okay? I'd like to see you do better."

"Look," began Sam, "I'm glad you figured out somewhere to stay, but I've been thinking about all this Malifex business. I don't want to get involved. I can't believe it's really anything to do with me—I'm just here on vacation. It's all just coincidence. I mean, what if we'd decided to go to Cornwall instead?"

"Ah," replied Amergin with a knowing smile, "but you didn't."

"Anyway. I don't want to get involved. I'm going to spend the rest of the break with my parents, doing . . . well . . . vacation stuff. Sorry." And with that he turned and strode back to the cottage.

From the bushes that lined the farm's entrance, two pairs of green eyes watched him without blinking. After the cottage door closed, sleekly muscled, black bodies pushed through the undergrowth, seeming to evaporate like smoke and were gone.

The next morning, Sam awoke to the muffled sound of voices from downstairs. He threw on some clothes and headed to the kitchen, running his fingers through his tousled hair. Turning the corner at the bottom of the stairs, he froze in the kitchen doorway. There was Mr. Halifax, chatting to his parents at the breakfast table. As before, his parents seemed oblivious to the leering face of the Malifex, as he dropped out of their conversation and turned toward Sam.

The deep voice sounded in his head once again, "It seems our little chat yesterday has gone unheeded. My agents saw you with that buffoon Amergin and the girl. It would seem that a more tangible warning is needed." The Malifex turned back to Sam's parents and clicked his fingers, then he rose and headed for the door.

Before he left, he turned to Sam. "It's merely a warning.

I have been remarkably forbearing so far. I must be getting sentimental in my old age." He chuckled and left.

Sam looked at his parents, who had become curiously still. He ran over and shook his mother's arm, but she didn't move. In fact, she had gone completely rigid. Sam pushed her hard, but she and Sam's father were frozen, locked in place as if turned to stone.

chapter 7

Sam ran out of the house and across the farmyard to Charly's cottage, where he banged furiously on the door. Charly's mother answered. "Oh, hello there," she said, "you must be Sam. Charly's told me about you. Did you want to speak with her?"

Sam merely nodded, too full of emotion to speak. He was ushered inside and after a moment Charly appeared.

"Oh, it's you," she began. "I thought you didn't want anything to do with us."

"Get Amergin—quickly." Sam demanded. "It's my parents!"

Charly was about to ask questions, but something in Sam's expression made her rush to comply. As soon as Amergin appeared, Sam shouted, "Come on!" and set off across the farmyard, Charly and Amergin following at a run.

They burst into the kitchen, hot on Sam's heels, and at once it was obvious that something was wrong. Sam's parents sat where he had left them, rigid and unseeing.

Amergin hurried over and began to examine them. "Who did this, child?" he asked gravely.

"It was him, the Malifex!" Sam blurted out. "He calls

himself Mr. Halifax. He met my parents yesterday at the castle. While he was talking to them, he somehow spoke to me in my head and told me to abandon my quest. Then, because I spoke to you last night, he came here this morning and did this." He looked at Amergin with panic in his eyes. "What has he done? Can you help them?"

Amergin moved from one frozen figure to the other, waving his hands in strange gestures and muttering. Then he said, "I cannot, my friend. His power is far greater than I had feared, but your parents are not harmed. He has merely removed them from the stream of time."

"But how do we get them back?" demanded Sam. "We can't leave them like this."

Amergin sat down in one of the remaining chairs at the breakfast table and said, "There is only one way. Complete your quest. Defeat the Malifex, and they will be freed from his power."

"What quest?" wailed Sam, "I'm not on a quest! I tried to tell him that, but he wouldn't listen."

"Your quest began," replied Amergin, "when you woke me from my sleep. If the Malifex sought to deter you from your path, he has miscalculated, for now your only hope of freeing your parents is to go forward. We should take comfort that he can make such mistakes."

Charly, who had been watching them with concern, spoke up. "Amergin has spent a lot of time talking to my mother, looking at old books and maps. He can help you."

"Indeed, my young friend," agreed Amergin, "my sole purpose here is to help you. It has always been thus, down the ages. Arthur had Merlin; you have me."

"You mean," said Sam, "that King Arthur was the last one to defeat the Malifex?"

"Indeed. Each time the forces of darkness rise, a champion comes who must fight to defeat them. You are that champion, and I was appointed to guide you, as Merlin guided Arthur. Although, I have to say, Merlin had many years to train Arthur. Oh, well," he said briskly, "a challenge will stretch us both."

"I don't want to be stretched!" complained Sam. "I want my parents back, then I want things to go back to normal!"

"In that case," said Amergin, getting to his feet, "we had better get started."

They left Sam's parents at the breakfast table, Sam reluctantly extracting the keys from his father's pocket and locking the cottage door behind them. Charly's mother was firing pots in the kiln at the back of the cottage, so they headed for the study and the collection of books that she and Amergin had been consulting. The study was lined with dark wooden shelves, glass-fronted and packed with books, but with many empty spaces bearing testimony to the previous day's activity. The missing volumes were piled in precarious heaps on every level surface, including the floor. Several were still open on the big oak desk by the window. Old botanical prints and strange masks, depicting faces adorned with leaves, decorated the small areas of visible wall space. Bunches of drying herbs hung from the rafters, and a large ginger cat was asleep on the window sill.

Installing himself cross-legged in one of the more comfortable armchairs, Amergin began, "It is clear that you possess a certain degree of power, my friend, and given time we could, through training, build on this power. Time, however, is something we do not have in abundance. So, if you are to stand any chance against the Malifex, we will need help. There are various items of power that the wise have used down the ages to combat the forces of darkness. Some, like the sword Excalibur, are lost to us. Others remain but are hidden. The more of these items we can obtain, the more your natural powers will be enhanced."

"So where do we look?" asked Charly. "And what are we looking for?"

"Wait a minute," interrupted Sam, "this is my problem. There's no point in you getting dragged into it. It could be dangerous."

"Don't be dense," replied Charly, "I've got a wizard staying in my guest room. I've already been dragged into it. You said the Malifex had seen you talking to us, so this is as much my problem now as yours."

Sam couldn't think of an argument and was secretly relieved that Charly wanted to join in.

"The principal items of power," continued Amergin, "are mentioned in the song that you and I, Charly, were discussing yesterday."

"Amergin wrote this song," Charly explained to Sam. "It was number one in the charts two thousand years ago. I'll tell you about it later."

Amergin looked slightly offended but continued. "As I was saying, the song mentions them thus: I am the spear that rears for blood, I am the tear the sun lets fall.

"The spear, or rather the spearhead, is a powerful weapon against the dark, forged long ago of silver and engraved with symbols of power. Thus its maker placed an enchantment on it that it might penetrate any armor or spell of protection. It has been called by some the Spear of Destiny, for whoever wields it, for good or ill, holds the fate of the land in their hands.

"The Tear of the Sun is a gold amulet that greatly enhances the power of the wearer. It is said to have fallen to earth from the sky and so is also called the lapis ex coelis—the stone from heaven. There are other items of varying usefulness. For instance: I am the stag of seven tines refers to a helmet, the Helm of Herne the Hunter. It is crowned with the antlers of a stag and gives the wearer protection against attacks, both physical and magical."

"What are tines?" asked Sam.

"They are the points, or branches, of a stag's antlers," explained Amergin.

"And who's Herne the Hunter?" It was Charly's turn for a question.

"A figure from ancient legend," Amergin said, "an aspect of Cernunnos, the god of the underworld. He leads the Wild Hunt and is said to appear, crowned with antlers and festooned with chains, in times of great need."

"Hey," said Sam, brightening up, "this is kind of like a computer game!"

"Oh, here we go!" sighed Charly.

"No, listen, it is. It's like power-ups—health bonuses, armor bonuses—that you have to collect before you stand a chance against the level boss."

Charly and Amergin looked blank.

"The bad guy at the end of the game," explained Sam.

"If only it were a game," sighed Amergin.

"So, where can we find these power-ups?" asked Sam, who now seemed quite optimistic.

"Therein lies the problem," replied Amergin. "They were placed in certain well-known sites of power, but even a brief glance at these books," he gestured at the desk, "shows that much has changed."

"In what way?" asked Sam.

"Well, our greatest enemy seems to have been greed. Over the centuries, many of the sites have been raided by treasure seekers, perhaps sent by the Malifex, although people can do evil enough without his guidance. For instance, the Tear of the Sun was placed on the breast of a great king, who was buried in a tomb not far from here." He spread out a map on the desk. It was upside down. He picked it up and tried to wrangle the accordian-like folds back together, without success. With great rustling and crackling, the wizard wrestled with the expanse of paper, growing redder and redder in the face. Finally, he exclaimed, "Oh, confound the thing!" and threw it down on the desk. Charly deftly picked it up, folded it back into shape, turned it around, and reopened it.

Smoothing the map out on the desktop, Charly pointed, "Just here, look. King's Barrow, outside Stoborough."

"However," continued Amergin, "this book of local history recounts that the tomb was robbed in 1762 and that the thieves were caught and taken to Wareham to be tried by the local judge. Rumor has it that they found some item of great value, but when they were caught, all they were carrying were a few bronze cups and copper brooches. The thieves were convicted and were sentenced to be hung. All that could be learned from them before they died was that the bulk of their find 'had been given into the care of old Harry.'" Amergin turned to Sam. "So there the trail goes cold. This Harry was no doubt an accomplice of theirs, who was never caught. The Tear of the Sun, if that is indeed what they found, could be anywhere now."

"So, what do we do?" asked Sam.

"Ah, my friend, what indeed? I fear we may have to forego the tear and choose an easier target."

"We could go to the Records Office in Wareham," suggested Charly, "and look for people called Harold."

"Oooh, yeah," snapped Sam, "I bet there aren't many of those!"

"Well, you come up with a better plan, Einstein!"

"Children, children," Amergin broke in, "squabbling will not solve the problem. I will continue to consult your mother's library." He wandered over to the bookshelves and was soon lost in thought. Charly stuck out her tongue at Sam and threw herself into an armchair, arms around her shins and knees against her chin.

Sam sat at the desk and gazed blankly at the map. He was fascinated by maps, could stare at them for hours, marveling at the strange place names. This particular example was absolutely swarming with barrows, tumuli, and strip lynchets, whatever they were. Idly, Sam picked up a trinket from the desk near his right hand, a piece of clear crystal on a slender silver chain, presumably a necklace belonging to Charly or her mother. He fiddled with it as he stared at the map, seeking any clue that might help them find the Tear of the Sun. He was holding the necklace by the chain, swinging the crystal in circles over the map, when he noticed something strange. He shuddered and dropped the necklace as though it had given him an electric shock. Then, despite his apprehension, he picked it up and began to swing it again.

"Hey, guys," he said in a small voice. "Er, Amergin? Charly? You might want to see this."

"What is it?" asked Charly, appearing by his shoulder.

"Watch." Sam began to swing the piece of crystal in circles over the map.

"Wow!" gasped Charly, sarcastically. "That's amazing! You can swing it around and around! Can you make it go the other way?"

"Don't be dumb!" sighed Sam. "It was doing something weird."

"Somebody's doing something weird," muttered Charly.

"Describe what happened," said Amergin in a patient voice.

"Well," began Sam, "I was just swinging it around in circles, like this, and I noticed that it was being pulled, as if by a magnet or something, but it's crystal—a magnet shouldn't affect it."

"And what were you thinking about, while you were doing this?" asked the wizard.

"Well, about the tear, I suppose. I was looking for clues."

"Try it again. And this time, think about the tear."

Sam began to swing the crystal in loose circles over the map, trying to remember what had been going through his mind last time. He had been looking at place names, that was right, and then at all the barrows and tumuli. Then he had started thinking about the tear, and the king in his barrow, and the mysterious Harry.

"Oh, wow!" exclaimed Charly, with no trace of sarcasm this time. Sam looked at the crystal. It was no longer circling but hung at an unnatural angle. Like a dog pulling at its leash, it was straining toward the eastern side of the map.

"It's pointing toward Studland," said Charly, peering more closely, "and Ballard Down."

The ridge of the Purbeck Hills behind the farm ran from its gap at Corfe Castle eastward as far as Brenscombe Hill, then became Nine Barrow Down, where they had awoken Amergin, before being broken by another gap. The final section, between this gap and the sea, was called Ballard Down, and there on its broad summit were the words King Barrow.

"There's another King Barrow!" said Charly excitedly. "Perhaps it wasn't the one near Stoborough that was looted after all!"

"And look there!" exclaimed Sam. "Old Harry!" He pointed. At the extreme easterly end of the ridge, where Ballard Down thrust into Poole Bay like the prow of a ship, were the words Old Harry and Old Harry's Wife.

"Of course!" Charly slapped her forehead. "Why didn't I think of that? Old Harry is the big stack of chalk, where this ridge behind us sticks out into the sea. There are lots of natural arches and chalk columns and things—Old

Harry and his wives. The thieves might not have been talking about a person at all. 'The treasure was given into the care of Old Harry.' They must've hidden it there."

"Do you know," replied Amergin with respect in his voice, "I think you might be right?"

"Okay," said Sam, "what are we waiting for? Let's go!"

They told Charly's mother that they were off to do some sightseeing, and, after she had made them sandwiches and a thermos of tea, they set off over Brenscombe Hill. They retraced the route they had taken after their encounter with the beasts of the Malifex, dropping down from the crest of the ridge onto the road at its foot. They sat down to wait at the bus stop where they had been dropped off two days earlier. Before them, the land dropped away to dark pine forest, and beyond it, pale in the distance, lay a vast wilderness of heathland. They sat in silence, each lost in thought, until Charly, glancing to her left, saw the bus approaching. They jumped to their feet, grabbed their packs, and flagged it down.

The driver dropped them off in the village of Studland, and, after some thought, Charly chose a narrow path that climbed up through a tunnel of overhanging trees and eventually brought them into open farmland on the top of Ballard Down. From here, the path ran along the edge of a plowed field, beyond which the cliffs dropped abruptly to Studland Bay. The sun blazed down, and a welcome breeze blew in from the sea. The blue-green water of the bay was crisscrossed with the white wakes of jet skis and speedboats. A few scattered tourist groups were using the path, stopping now and then to gaze out over the bay.

Emerging from a stretch of scrub and low trees, Sam, Charly, and Amergin found themselves in an area of wind-stunted gorse bushes that thinned toward the cliff edge. A handful of tourists were sitting on the grass or peering over the edge at the drop below. Charly gestured toward a point where the cliff edge made a sharp right angle, and the three of them headed where she had indicated. Sam gave a low whistle.

In front of them, the clifftop came to a point, becoming narrower and narrower until it formed a knife-edged ridge barely wide enough to walk along. To either side, the cliffs dropped vertically to the sea below. Toward its end, the ridge dipped slightly, made a final short climb like a ramp, and then seemed to stop. Beyond, separated by about seventy-five feet of fresh air, was Old Harry.

Old Harry was a rough block of dazzling white chalk, the same height as the cliffs and topped off with a patch of grass, like an ill-fitting wig. The sides were sheer, and the nearest part of the stack, which tapered toward them, was pierced at the base by a tunnel, through which the sea moved back and forth. Beyond Old Harry, just visible over his shoulder, was a round, slender column of chalk, separated from him by a further gap—Old Harry's Wife.

"What are we going to do?" asked Sam. "How are we going to get across?"

"I fear," replied Amergin, "that the path between here and Old Harry has collapsed since our thieving friend was here. Looking on the bright side, whatever he hid there should have remained undisturbed ever since." They peered over the edge of the cliff. At sea level, between the cliff where they stood and the base of Old Harry, was a rough mound of chalk rubble, eroded by the sea but presumably representing the remains of the link between Old Harry and the mainland.

"Well," said Charly with a sigh, "that's that."

"Ah, have faith, child! I am not entirely without power. Let me see."

With that, Amergin began to wander around the headland, pausing now and then to peer around him. He was beginning to attract curious stares from the handful of tourists. "Oh, bother it!" he muttered. "I hate an audience." He put his hand to his forehead, fingers at one temple, thumb at the other, and began to mutter under his breath. Suddenly, the various groups of people began to pack up their belongings and wander off. A couple who had just emerged from the path through the nearby scrub suddenly stopped in their tracks, turned without a word, and headed back the way they had come with blank eyes and expressionless faces. Soon, the three of them had the headland to themselves.

"Yes, yes," announced Amergin after a few moments, "this should be possible. The land remembers." Sam and Charly looked at each other, puzzled. "Come!" he announced and strode over to the prow of the headland. He stopped at a point just before the land narrowed to form its final ridge and knelt on the ground. "The land remembers its former shape," he explained. "I will try to recreate a time when there was a bridge over to Old Harry. Trust in me." He placed his hands on the ground at either side, fingers spread. "Go on, Sam," he instructed. "Walk across."

"But it isn't working. There's nothing there," complained Sam.

"I cannot make it visible. It is taking all my power just to make it solid. Have faith, and do not look down."

With a last nervous glance at Amergin, Sam set off along the path. It narrowed to such an extent that he could barely have stood on it with his feet side by side. He felt like he was on a tightrope. The path dipped slightly, then rose again. At the top of the rise, he stopped. The ground plunged away in front of him to the rocks below.

"Go on!" called Amergin from behind him. "And hurry—I cannot sustain this forever."

Sam put one foot in front of him and was astonished to find that it stopped a short distance above what appeared to be the ground. There was something solid but invisible there. He put his weight on the leading foot, then brought his other foot around and put it down, again on what appeared to be thin air. With growing confidence, he set off toward Old Harry.

About halfway across the invisible bridge, he glanced down at his feet and froze. The absurdity of his situation hit him like a hammer blow, leaving him breathless. He was standing in midair, almost a hundred feet above the sea and rocks, with a breeze swirling around him. He screwed his eyes shut and stood there panting.

"Hurry!" cried Amergin.

"Come on, Sam," shouted Charly. When he still did not move, Charly jumped up and ran after him.

"Be careful, child!" shouted Amergin. She traversed the visible section of the path quickly and then, with the briefest hesitation, went into the void. Coming up behind Sam, she put a hand on each of his shoulders.

"Come on, let's get this over with. Right foot first," she growled in his ear.

"I can't!" he mumbled.

"Oh, yes, you can," she replied, "or you'll have me to contend with. Right foot." Sam slid his right foot forward. "Good. Now the left." He did as instructed. Slowly at first but gaining speed, the two of them marched forward, Charly's hands still on Sam's shoulders. A faint cry of "Left! Right! Left! Right!" drifted back to Amergin, who managed to smile despite gritted teeth.

Finally, Charly and Sam reached visible ground beneath their feet. Sam fell to his knees. Back on the mainland, Amergin let his head drop forward, beads of sweat dripping off his nose.

"Okay," said Charly, "what now?" She sat on the grass next to where Sam had collapsed.

"Don't know," he panted at her.

"Well, you're the hero. Think of something. Be heroic!"

Sometimes Charly gave him an almost overwhelming urge to scream.

"Okay," he flopped back on to the grass next to her, "imagine, you're on the run with stolen goods. You've climbed over here—the land bridge would be visible but still pretty scary—and you need somewhere to hide a small package. Let's assume he didn't have time to dig a hole."

"Why?" asked Charly.

"Because if we assume that he dug a hole, then the package could be anywhere around here, and we haven't got a shovel, so we would have to spend the rest of the day scratching the dirt with our fingers."

"Hmmmm . . . I'm not convinced . . . but go on."

"Look, if he could get over here, then so could anyone who followed him, and they could have brought shovels. He needed a natural hiding place in a hurry. He needed a hole or a cave of some sort."

"Well, anything like that would be on the sides, rather than on the top, where the bare chalk is."

"Exactly," replied Sam, "and somewhere where it couldn't be seen from the mainland."

"So, the opposite side from the land bridge?"

"Come on!" Sam jumped to his feet, pulling Charly up after him and headed for the far edge of the stack. They stopped near the edge, with a dizzying drop in front of them. Old Harry's Wife faced them across a gap.

"So, somewhere down here?" asked Charly.

"I suppose so," replied Sam. "Just hope it hasn't crumbled away. Well, here goes." He dropped to the grass, lay face down, and thrust one arm over the edge. Groping around revealed nothing but a crumbling face of chalk, so he shuffled along to an area that had previously been out of reach and began again. After several changes of position, he announced, "I think I can feel something, but I can't completely reach it. He would have had longer arms than me. Grab my feet."

Charly lay down on the grass behind him and grabbed him by the ankles. He crept farther forward, bending at the waist until most of his upper body was hanging over the cliff edge. "Don't let go. I think I can feel something."

His hand had found a rough hole in the cliff face, and, at full stretch, his fingers crept inside it. Straining until he thought his shoulder would dislocate, he managed to grasp a piece of what felt like rough cloth between his index and middle fingers. He pulled it forward slightly until he could get a firm grasp, then shouted, "Pull me back, Charly! I think I've found something!"

Collapsing back on to the springy turf, Sam waved a small bundle of rough sackcloth at Charly and whooped in triumph. His arm was covered in white chalk dust, as was the package. "Let's take a look."

Charly came to sit beside him as he unfolded the cloth. Inside was another bundle wrapped in a softer cloth, which may have once been dyed but was now bleached with time and chalk dust. They glanced at each other, then Sam removed the second layer. Charly gasped as she saw a gleam of light. Nestled in Sam's palm was a tear-shaped golden pendant, intricately decorated with engraved images. Sam could see a leaping fish, a hawk with wings spread, a flower. A gold chain passed through a hole at the pendant's narrow end.

He turned to Charly. "Looks like we did it." She smiled. "Let's get back." He wrapped the amulet back up in its layers of cloth.

They returned to the landward side of Old Harry and waved the package in the air at Amergin. He waved back, then dropped to his knees as before.

"Come!" he cried. "I grow tired." They stepped gingerly back on to the invisible bridge, with Charly holding Sam's shoulders as before. Flushed with his success, he found the return journey much easier. They had passed the halfway point when Charly felt Sam's shoulders tense in her grasp.

"Amergin!" he shouted. "Behind you!" Peering around him, Charly could see two black, feline shapes converging on Amergin's kneeling figure, one from either side.

Amergin looked around. "Quickly!" he called. "I cannot hold them and the bridge!"

Sam glanced down at the sea beating against the foot of the cliffs, far, far below.

chapter 8

Sam looked frantically from Amergin to the two Dhouls, which were converging on the wizard rapidly but cautiously. "Come on!" he shouted to Charly and set off toward the clifftop as quickly as he dared, conscious of the narrow, invisible path beneath his feet. It was clear, however, that unless they ran, which would be suicidal given their precarious location, the cats would reach Amergin before they were safely on the mainland.

"Sam!" Charly called from behind him, "The amulet!" He looked stupidly down at the package in his hand, then realized what Charly had in mind. The wizard had told them that the amulet greatly enhanced the power of whoever wore it.

With a bellow of "Amergin!" he hurled the package with all his strength toward where the wizard knelt. Amergin turned and caught it neatly, ripped off the covering layers of cloth, and put the chain around his neck.

Sam recoiled from his throw, teetering on the invisible bridge. Unable to keep his balance, he took a step back and felt, to his horror, nothing beneath his foot. For a stretched moment he hung, windmilling his arms. Charly made a grab for him and succeeded in catching him by one wrist as his feet slipped off the invisible rock, and he slithered toward the crashing waves below.

Back on the mainland, the Dhouls had drawn close to Amergin, taking care to keep to either side, dividing his attention. Suddenly, there was a shimmer in the air, and the black cats were replaced by two dark figures, tall and skeletally thin, wielding slender black rods. At the tip of each rod, a sphere of green fire appeared. Moving in unison, like sinister puppets, they raised the rods behind their heads. The spheres of light detached themselves and hovered in the air, each attached to the tip of its rod by a thin filament of green energy. Like some kind of unearthly whip, the glowing cords lashed back and forth through the air, crackling and sparking.

Suddenly, Amergin heard a cry and turned just in time to see Sam slip from the land bridge and hang in midair, Charly clinging to one arm. Taking advantage of the wizard's distraction, the servants of the Malifex moved to strike, two balls of evil radiance arching through the air toward him. Quickly, he made a gesture before him, and a faint dome of light became visible. The balls of light rebounded, spitting and sparking on their glowing cords, but the force of their impact had knocked Amergin to his knees.

Sam looked up and was astonished to see his fingers clenched in thin air, his fingertips pressed white and bloodless, the tendons straining. He could feel the rough texture of chalk beneath his hand and struggled to convince himself that there was something there, bearing his weight. Charly was pulling on his other arm. "Try and swing your legs up," she grated. She hauled at his wrist as he scrabbled to find a hold on the invisible rock. Then, one foot lodged in an unseen crevice, and he struggled back onto the level top of the land bridge. Looking to the mainland, he saw Amergin down on his knees, the Tear of the Sun clasped in one hand.

At that moment, the Dhouls struck again, and Amergin threw all his strength into the dome of unearthly force that surrounded him. His power and attention diverted, the memory of the land bridge began to fade, and Sam felt the invisible ground beneath his feet melt away. Flailing one arm behind him, he grabbed Charly by the hand as they plummeted toward the rocks and the swirling sea below. As the wind screamed past his ears, Sam felt a prickling sensation all over his body, as if his skin were crawling with ants. Eyes shut tight, he braced himself for the impact. When it came, he whimpered despite himself as the air rushed out from between his clenched teeth. But something was wrong. There was no pain, no splintering rock or cold seawater, just soft, dry grass beneath his cheek. Opening one eye, he saw Charly staring at him in wonder. They were on the clifftop.

"I don't know how you did that, buddy," she gasped, "but that was . . . good. That was definitely . . . okay."

Sam heard a harsh grunt and looked over to where Amergin was locked in battle with the Malifex's dark servants. The Dhouls drew back their rods and prepared to strike again, but at the first sign of movement, Sam bellowed, "No!" and they paused, distracted for a moment. Amergin, seeing his chance, raised his arms, fingers spread. A blaze of light erupted from each of his outflung hands and crackled toward the two thin figures. Each became enveloped in a weblike network of blue light. They seemed to writhe in a series of grotesque shapes, growing smaller by the second until, with a brief flare of blue-white light and a dwindling shriek, they vanished.

Charly and Sam scrambled to their feet and ran to Amergin's side.

"Wow!" exclaimed Sam. "That was excellent!"

"Are they . . . dead?" asked Charly.

"No, no, child. Even with the amulet, I have not the power to destroy them utterly. They are weakened, dispersed, and will skulk back to their master's side, without form for a time. But while ever he endures, so do they."

He brightened and looked at them with a sudden smile. "This, however, I cannot keep, for it is yours." He took the amulet from around his neck and handed it to Sam. "It is best that you do not wear it unless in need."

"What now?" asked Sam, feeling confident with the weight of the amulet in his pocket. "What should we look for next?"

"Ah, my friend!" exclaimed Amergin. "We have been lucky. Do not assume that such luck will hold. We should retire for this day, make our plans. Our next target, I feel, should be the Helm of Herne."

After an uneventful bus journey and a pleasant walk back over Brenscombe Hill, they arrived at the farm. As they drew near, Sam grew quiet. The sight of the buildings nestled in the trees reminded him of the motionless figures of his parents inside.

"Come on," said Charly, sensing his mood, "we're doing well so far. We've got the amulet, those two cats, or whatever they are, got their butts kicked—we're getting there."

"Getting where, though?" asked Sam. "I still don't know what I'm supposed to do. One minute I'm on vacation, the next I'm up to my neck in all this. Running around with wizards, walking on thin air, chasing treasure. Only Amergin seems to know what's going on, and sometimes I'm not even sure about that. None of this seems real, but I know it's not a game. In games, if you die, you just start again."

Charly tried to look reassuring. "Well, when we get back home, let's see if we can't get some more information out of you-know-who." She gestured at Amergin, who was striding across the farmyard toward his adopted home.

The Malifex paced across the deep carpet of his office on the third floor of a gray stone building in central London. A large, rectangular table in the center of the room held a richly colored map that showed the British Isles in contoured relief. The Malifex looked at the southwestern corner of the map, where, amid the gray expanse of the desolate tableland of Dartmoor, was a single, small patch of emerald green. He peered closely at this last remnant of wildwood, the only area of its kind remaining on the map. Frowning, he straightened and crossed to his massive, polished desk, where he sank into the black leather of a revolving chair.

A few minutes later, the Malifex looked up from his

paperwork at the blinking light of a telephone. Lifting the receiver, he snapped, "Halifax."

After a few moments, he nodded.

"Good, good," he rumbled. "Buy it and bulldoze it."

He listened for a few moments more. "I don't care if it is protected, it will have to go. We will plant a new wood somewhere to replace it. The need for this road scheme is quite clear—nothing will be allowed to stand in its way . . . No, money is no object. Exactly . . . buy it and raze it to the ground."

He replaced the receiver and pressed a button beneath his desk. Over by the door, solid bolts could be heard slamming into place. The oak-paneled wall behind his desk slid away to reveal a bank of video screens.

Picking up a remote control, the Malifex leaned back and began to press buttons. One by one, the screens flickered into life. A mounted camera showed eight lanes of stationary traffic in a haze of exhaust fumes. A documentary described the problems faced by families living in the inner-city. The camera tracked slowly past boarded-up shops where children huddled in the doorways, shivering in the litter. A computer-enhanced satellite photograph showed land use. The cities and towns were a brooding purple, the road network blood-red, like veins and capillaries, joining black clots of heavy industry.

As more and more screens blinked into life, the babble of voices and the roar of machinery rose to a crescendo. The Malifex threw back his head and howled with laughter, arms hanging limply by the sides of his chair.

Suddenly, he grunted, as if with pain, and jumped to his

feet. Clicking off his wall of screens, he paced toward the center of the room in the sudden silence, and, as he walked, his outline shimmered and blurred. Instead of the smart suit and tie, he was clad in dark robes that trailed across the rich carpet.

In the middle of the room, he stopped. The lights had dimmed, and dusk was falling outside the windows. The Malifex raised his hands from his sides, palms upward and fingers curled, and gazed toward the ceiling. Slowly, before him, two patches of darkness seemed to condense from the gloom and float, writhing, a short distance above the floor.

The Malifex let his hands fall back and gazed at the two swirling clouds, shaking his head sadly. The twin shadows seemed to grow more agitated under his gaze, fawning like whipped dogs.

"You fools!" screamed the Malifex and made a gesture that sent the dark clouds flying to the corners of the room, where they slammed against the walls and sank to the floor, merging with the more natural shadows.

"Beaten by that bungler Amergin. I can see that my presence is required once more."

With that, the Malifex made a complex gesture in the air before him and seemed to melt into the carpet. Moments later, his dark spirit sped through the streets of London, heading for Dorset.

≈

Charly's mother had gone to Wareham for the day, so Charly let them in and put on the tea kettle. Then, with steaming mugs of tea, they settled into the mismatched assortment of chairs in the study. "Amergin," began Charly, glancing at Sam for support, "we were wondering about this business. . . . You haven't really told us very much about what we're up against. Don't you think that would be useful, keeping in mind we seem to be in a fair amount of trouble?" Amergin looked from one to the other, then sighed.

"You are right. I had thought to protect you, for there is much to fear, but you will need all the knowledge you can gather for the task ahead. Ask, and I will try to answer."

"Well, where do we start?" asked Sam. "We don't know anything, really. For instance, all this stuff about the Malifex and the forces of darkness. Apart from him threatening me and those two cat things wandering around, what exactly is the problem? What are we trying to stop him from doing?"

"A perceptive question, my friend." Amergin settled himself more comfortably. "Each time the forces of evil rise, the threat takes a different form. Always the Malifex spreads his lies and bends the hearts of humans to his will from some position of authority. He is never the leader but is often the power behind the leader, influencing policy and whispering poison in the ear of whoever is in charge. His aim is ever to turn the thoughts of the people to darkness and destruction, and always there are many who are more than willing to listen to his lies. I have spent some time since I awoke searching for his scent in this land, but these are complex times. So many people, so many places for him to hide." Amergin sighed.

"He told my father that he was something in the civil

service," said Sam. "That's part of the government. He could be an adviser or something."

"Ahh," replied Amergin, "just the sort of place one would expect to find him. From there, he can remain faceless but influence much."

"So, what do you think he's planning to do?" asked Charly.

"I have read your newspapers and watched this thing, this television, that you spoke of. Much of what I saw and read I did not understand, but I understood enough to know that his work is nearly complete."

"How do you mean?" asked Sam, with growing fear.

"Remember," replied Amergin, "that I told you about the dark and the light and how there cannot be one without the other?" They nodded. "Good and evil are constantly shifting their balance, and, from what I have seen, that balance has shifted far in favor of the Malifex. Chaos and destruction have overwhelmed the forces of growth and rebirth. This land is choked with cities, its air and water poisoned, its forests felled, all at the hands of people. The old ways are forgotten by all but a few." He glanced at Charly. "When the last fragments of the ancient wildwood that once covered this land are lost, his victory will be complete. We are all that stands in his way."

"So what do we have to do?" asked Sam in a small voice.

"Simple," responded Amergin. "Defeat him, or all beauty and goodness will pass away, and his dominion will last forever."

"That's all?" said Sam and fell silent.

"Our peril is now great," Amergin continued. "He

knows that we are the only threat to his plan, hence his presence here. He would not show himself openly unless he felt victory was close. He will be watching our every move, and his agents will be all around."

"I thought those two cat guys were his agents?" enquired Charly. "They won't be bothering us for a while."

"His power is at its peak. It will not be long before the Dhouls are restored to their bodies, but they are only chief among his servants. More often he works his evil through humans, those drawn by their nature to do his will. We must be vigilant."

"So, this helmet thing—how do we find that?" asked Sam.

"That is less of a mystery than the Tear of the Sun," Amergin answered, "although not without its problems. Its location is well documented; we need only follow the directions."

"And what are they?" asked Charly.

"A verse," Amergin replied, "known well to the wise and recorded in several of your mother's books, although the authors could only speculate as to its meaning." He closed his eyes, as if searching his memories, and recited:

> At the Castle of the Maiden,
> The meeting of the ways,
> Stand atop the temple
> And cast around your gaze.
> If the Hunter you would find,
> The old ways summon forth.
> His horse and helm lie to the south
> But Herne lies to the north.

"Some directions!" said Sam. "It's not exactly 'turn left at the traffic lights, then take the second right.'"

"But it will suffice," said Amergin. "The only problem is one of transportation. The Castle of the Maiden lies to the west of Durnovaria, which is some miles from here."

"Sorry," Charly interrupted, "but I've never heard of it, and I know the area pretty well."

"Oh, confound it. I expect the name has changed, like everything else. Where's the map?" Amergin rummaged around in the clutter on the desk, eventually pulling out a well-worn map of the area. "Ah, yes. Here we are—Dorchester. Although what was wrong with Durnovaria, I'm sure I don't know. The Romans were terribly good at names, I always thought . . . and roads. Excellent roads."

"Yes, that's all great," said Sam, "but how are we going to get all the way to Dorchester?"

"I think it is time," replied Amergin, "that I taught you a few tricks of the Craft, but not now. We will wait until dark."

chapter 9

Charly's Uncle Pete eased off his boots and sank into his favorite armchair, wriggling his toes in front of the fire. A few minues later, his wife, Janet, bustled in with a cup of tea. "Dinner's in about half an hour," she said as she collapsed into a chair on the opposite side of the hearth. "How did it go today?"

"Not bad," replied Pete, after a moment's thought. "Aye, not bad at all, to be honest. Young George's coming along okay. We'll make a stockman of him yet. And the cow with mastitis, you know the one?"

"Hawthorn."

Pete smiled affectionately at his wife. "Aye, Hawthorn, although how you can remember the names of fifty head of cattle, I'll never know. Anyway, Hawthorn seems to be on the mend, and I used the new forage harvester on Glebe Close. A good day's work." He closed his eyes and savored the warmth soaking into his fingers from the steaming mug. Suddenly, there was a knock at the door.

"Who can that be at this hour?" asked Janet, getting to her feet.

"You see to dinner, love. I'll answer it." Pete padded down the passageway in his stockinged feet.

Janet made her way to the kitchen, where an assortment of pots and pans bubbled and steamed on the old range. She fell into the absentminded rhythm of cooking, wandering from stove to sink to cupboard, prodding potatoes with the point of a knife, stirring, sipping, adding.

Pete hauled open the heavy front door and was surprised to see a tall, well-dressed stranger with jet-black hair slicked back from a high forehead. Piercing eyes looked out beneath dark brows. The well-tailored suit made Pete instantly wary. Only salespeople and representatives of the Ministry of Agriculture came to visit in suits.

"If you're selling something," Pete began, "we ain't interested . . . " Then he stopped . . . and screamed.

In the kitchen, Janet heard her husband's cry and, dropping her wooden spoon, ran down the passageway that led to the front of the house. When she reached the hallway, she saw a strange sight. A smartly dressed man stood in the open doorway. Her husband was facing him, and the stranger was holding his head—one hand on either cheek—peering intently into his face. As she approached, the man dropped his hands to his sides and looked at her with a smile.

Janet paused. "Pete?" she asked nervously. "Is everything . . . "

Pete turned to look at her, and she screamed, her hands flying to her mouth. His eyes were almost closed, and from between the lids wisps of pale green steam drifted into the cold night air. As the stranger pushed past her husband and moved toward her down the passageway, dark shadows rose up behind him. Janet started to back away. After three steps, she came up against a closed door. The man in the suit stopped before her and took her head gently in both hands. The shadows around him seemed to spread until all she could see was his calm, wise face hanging pale above her.

"Good evening," he said in a rich, musical voice. "I'm from the ministry."

She noticed his eyes, and her gaze was drawn into them, spiraling inward through flecks of hazel and green until she reached the darkness in the center. There she found black, eternal night, a sucking emptiness, hating light and life but hungry for them. The darkness was ancient, inhuman, and totally without mercy. Her mind recoiled in horror, and she remembered no more.

Sam was reluctant to spend any time alone in the cottage with his parents. Their silent presence disturbed him, and the threat of the Malifex was preying on his mind. Charly, sensing his unease, suggested that he sleep on the floor in Amergin's room and bundled him into the house while her mother was busy. When she was sure that her mother was asleep, Charly called on the others and together they crept out of the house.

In the moon-flooded farmyard, Amergin said, "Now would be a good time to wear the amulet." Sam took it from his pocket and placed the gold chain around his neck. "There is energy all around us," began Amergin, "that is the first thing to know. It flows through the land, the rocks, even the air around us. Certain places and objects concentrate this energy, which can be of great help to one who practices the Craft of the Wise, but an adept should be able to tap into the power wherever he—or she—may be. Now, my young friend, we need some means by which we may travel. Does anything come to your mind?"

"Er ... broomsticks?" said Sam after a pause.

"Oh, please!" sighed Charly.

"Well, I don't know—I'm new to this stuff."

"I fail to see how broomsticks would help us," said Amergin uncertainly. "I was thinking more of a change of form."

Charly looked thoughtful. "Bearing in mind what we're looking for," she began, "how about ... ?"

"My thoughts exactly," said Amergin with a smile.

"Join hands!" Sam was looking increasingly confused but did as he was instructed. "For this first time," Amergin turned to him, "I will take the lead. Take note; feel how the energy flows." Sam closed his eyes and, after a moment, felt a strange tickling sensation behind his eyes. Then a voice in his head, recognizable as Amergin, said "Hello? Ah, there you are. Now, follow my thoughts."

In the darkness behind his eyelids, Sam saw a vague animal form. Slowly, it grew more distinct, a slender-legged creature, with a high, proud head. He seemed, in his imagination, to rush suddenly toward the animal shape as if watching a film in fast forward. He caught a glimpse of a round, moist eye before a strange feeling of disorientation swept over him. The creature was no longer visible. Instead, a view of moonlit fields filled his vision. The cold air in his nostrils was laden with a dizzying range of subtle smells, and his ears picked up a symphony of tiny noises from the grass and hedgerows around him. There was a strange feeling of weight to the back of his head, a new kind of resistance as he turned his neck.

He shook his head from side to side to explore this new sensation and, from the corner of his eyes, saw figures to either side of him. To his right was a huge stag, crowned with a majestic set of antlers and sporting a shaggy mane of hair that ran down its neck and on to its shoulders. Its well-muscled forequarters gave way to sleek flanks and powerful hind legs. To his left was a smaller deer, without antlers. In its huge, liquid eye he saw himself reflected. "I am a stag of seven tines," he thought. The stag on his right threw back its head and bellowed, its breath steaming on the night air, then plunged forward into a gallop. Sam and Charly looked at each other briefly, then set off in pursuit.

The three of them sped across the moon-silvered landscape, leaping hedges and ditches, kicking up scraps of turf behind them. Sam felt as if electricity were running through him. His heart pounded like an engine in his chest, the cold night air swept past him, bringing with it smells—the lingering stink of gas as they crossed a road, the acrid musk of a fox, a tantalizing backdrop of lush grass. Through the night, the three of them ran, skirting villages, slowing to cross deserted roads, until at last, far beyond Corfe, they came to a meandering river valley, where Amergin turned west. Mile after mile, they galloped through rich riverside fields, leaping ditches and fences.

An orange glow began to grow in the sky before them; the town of Dorchester was near.

Some distance outside the town, Amergin slowed and followed a tributary of the river, which joined from the south. Their path was becoming increasingly hazardous as roads and a railroad line converged on the town. Several times they had to stop as cars tore through the darkness.

Finally, they saw a green hill rising abruptly in front of them. Amergin led them up the steep hillside until they stood side by side on the summit. There was a moment of spiraling disorientation, and they found themselves back in their own bodies. Sam felt as though he had a head cold—his hearing and sense of smell were suddenly reduced once more to their poor human levels.

"I know where this is!" exclaimed Charly. "It's Maiden Castle! I've been here with Mom."

"Indeed—the Castle of the Maiden. Humans have lived on this site for four millennia, but no more it would seem. Once a thriving town stood here, and these ridges that surround the hill were each crowned with great timbers to keep out the forces of the Malifex. Before that, the Romans had a temple dedicated to the goddess Diana, where we stand now." Amergin glanced at Charly. "It is a site of great significance."

"What happened?" asked Sam in a quiet voice.

"What did you say?" Amergin was puzzled.

"Last time," continued Sam. "What happened last time, when people lived here and tried to keep out the Malifex?"

"Ah, my friend, it is a long tale and a sad one. Suffice it to say that they failed and fell into darkness, and the

111

power of the Malifex held sway for a time. But always the wheel turns, and one comes who must defeat the forces of the dark. You are such a one."

They fell silent.

"So," asked Sam after a few moments, "what now?"

Charly frowned for a moment, then recited:

> At the Castle of the Maiden,
>
> The meeting of the ways,
>
> Stand atop the temple
>
> And cast around your gaze.

Well, we're here. What was the next part?" Amergin continued:

> If the Hunter you would find,
>
> The old ways summon forth.
>
> His horse and helm lie to the south
>
> But Herne lies to the north.

"So, what does that mean—the old ways summon forth?" asked Sam.

"As I have told you," explained Amergin, "this place has been a site of human habitation and great deeds for thousands of years. It is a meeting place of the old ways, the tracks and paths that are the arteries of this land."

There was silence, then Sam said, "Um, sorry but you lost me."

Amergin sighed. "The power I have spoken of, that which is the opposite of the evil of the Malifex, that into which we tap to practice the Craft, flows through this land in certain paths, connecting the great centers of power. All the important sites—the henges, the barrows, the stone circles—lie on such paths."

"Prehistoric ley lines!" exclaimed Charly. "I know about those."

"Unfamiliar words," replied Amergin, "but I sense that we talk of the same thing. Now, we must summon the ways into being, that we may follow the one we need." He gestured for them to join hands again.

They stood on the highest part of the castle, hands linked to form a human triangle, small against the dark of the night. Amergin threw back his head, eyes closed, and began to mutter under his breath. Sam felt a tingling in the soles of his feet, which quickly spread upward through his legs. The sensation built and built as Amergin's muttering reached a climax, then suddenly stopped. Sam was rather disappointed; he had been expecting something dramatic.

Then Charly shouted, "Look!"

He broke the circle of hands and turned to look where her gaze was fixed. Before them the landscape stretched out into the night as before, but now the sky was lit by an unearthly green glow, drowning out the lights of Dorchester. A network of glowing green lines crisscrossed the land, like rivers of emerald fire, most of them converging on the old fort where they stood. The Roman road they had crossed earlier was now a ruler-straight river of green light plunging to the southwest. To the west and east were narrower, winding ribbons of light, dotted with brighter points, like pearls on a necklace. Each bright dot represented a barrow, a tumulus, or a standing stone, and from each one a thin shaft of green radiance speared upward into the night. Maiden Castle was the hub of a vast, glowing spider's web of green energy, spreading out to the farthest limits of vision.

"It's beautiful!" gasped Charly.

"Behold the old ways of power!" cried Amergin. "We must choose our route."

"Didn't the rhyme say north?" asked Sam.

"If we sought Herne himself, our path would lie to the north," agreed Amergin. "His figure is carved in the chalk of a hillside, over yonder." He gestured behind them, beyond the lights of Dorchester, where they could just make out a bright shaft of light piercing the darkness. "However," continued Amergin, "we seek his horse and, in particular, his helm, which the rhyme tells us lie to the south."

Turning back, they followed Amergin's pointing finger. A single, straight line of green radiance ran in the direction he indicated, studded here and there with the glow from standing stones and ancient tombs. "Mark our path well in your minds, for we will not have this light to guide us as we travel."

"I suppose," said Charly, "that people will be starting to get suspicious by now. You must be able to see these lights for hundreds of miles."

"Only we can see the ways," replied Amergin, "as we are responsible for their summoning. There are others, however, who will have sensed such a display of power. The agents of the Malifex will be abroad."

"Is it far?" asked Sam.

"Not far," replied Amergin, "but now that we have drawn attention to ourselves we should make haste. I feel another change of shape is called for."

"Can I try this time?" Sam asked.

"Certainly. It will be good practice."

Sam took them each by the hand and closed his eyes. In his mind's eye, he pictured a small, reddish form with a pointed muzzle. He found this rather difficult, since he was working from TV documentaries and pictures in books, but then he felt a faint tickle in his skull, and the picture behind his eyes became clearer. He cast about him with his mind, tapping into the energy around him, then concentrated on the image and willed himself forward, experiencing again the rush of disorientation. Looking around, he felt a feeling of pride as he saw that he was flanked by a pair of foxes, one small and sleek, the other larger with a touch of gray around its muzzle.

With a yelp of excitement, Sam set off at a run, following the line of green light. As the three of them descended the hillside, however, the light faded and died. Sam's heightened fox senses allowed him to see clearly in the moonlight, and his nose was so flooded with information it made his head spin. The larger shape that was Amergin soon overtook him, and the three of them picked their way along a hedge that ran south and east. After skirting a small group of houses, they squeezed under the bottom rung of a gate and found themselves at the edge of the Roman road. On the far side, Sam noticed with a shudder the corpse of a fox lying on the verge, its fur matted with blood and dust and its eyes dull in the moonlight. He moved on quickly, down a slight bank and across a field of freshly turned earth. In front of them was another embankment, at the top of which was the railroad line. They ducked under the wire of the fence and crossed the tracks, Amergin in the lead.

Sam was puzzled by a strange, metallic slithering, a kind of sibilant ringing without obvious source. He paused, confused by the sound and the reek of tar and oil from the railroad cars. The sound seemed to be getting louder, so he forced himself to move on after the white tip of Amergin's disappearing tail. On the far side of the track, he stopped and looked back.

Like him, Charly had stopped in the middle of the line, hypnotized by the unearthly sound, which was now quite loud and had been joined by a dull rumble, sensed through the feet. Glancing to his right, he saw with horror the lights of a train approaching at top speed. Charly had seen it, too, but the lights, the strange sound, and the over-powering smell had left her paralyzed with confusion and mounting fear. She was directly in the path of the oncoming train, and there was no way Sam could reach her in time.

chapter 10

Sam realized that, in his panic, he had reverted to his human form and was standing at the side of the railroad line looking down at Charly. He pulled the Tear of the Sun from inside of his shirt, clasping it tightly in his hand. He had to think of something fast. The train was so close that Charly was ablaze in the glare of its headlights. Suddenly an image occurred to him. He clung to it desperately and focused all his attention on Charly, his eyes screwed shut and his hand gripping the amulet. Then he was buffeted by the shock wave of displaced air as the train thundered past.

When he dared to open his eyes again, the last few cars of the train were rattling past. There was no sign of Charly. He ran to the tracks and peered down at where she had last been standing. It was hard to see without a fox's night vision, but he could just make out a tiny round ball of fur. He closed his eyes for a second and, when he opened them again, there was Charly, gasping in the cold night air.

"Ohh," she panted, "ohh . . . that was . . . that was horrible! What happened? Why didn't it hit me?"

"I turned you into something else," replied Sam, sheepishly.

"What?" demanded Charly.

Sam muttered something inaudible.

"Sorry?" Charly was insistent. "I didn't catch that."

"I turned you into a hamster, all right?" Sam exclaimed in embarrassment. "I used to have a hamster. I know what they look like."

"Oh, very heroic!" exclaimed Charly. "Very Dungeons and Dragons!"

"I think our young friend showed remarkable resourcefulness," said Amergin, emerging from the darkness in human form. "You are growing in power, young Sam. There is yet hope."

"Were you watching?" asked Sam.

"I was ready to help if the need arose," admitted Amergin, "but you did admirably on your own."

"You helped back there at the fort, didn't you?" Sam continued. "I felt you in my head."

"Well, yes. A little. You were heading the right way, but the image in your mind, well, it was the most . . . er . . . unusual fox I had ever seen. I felt a little guidance was called for, otherwise who knows what you might have turned us into? And now, I think, it is time we resumed our journey."

Suddenly they were in fox shape again, stealing across the fields in the moonlight.

Meanwhile, in the silent streets of Corfe village, two black shapes moved through the darkness, slinking from shadow to shadow. A stray dog, making its nightly round of the village garbage cans, paused and sniffed the air. A faint hint of something reached its nose, something that it had never smelled before. The smell said predator. The dog stopped, growling deep in its throat, and crept stiff-legged back into the shadows as the two strange creatures padded by. It was approaching midnight.

The two huge cats made their way to the top of the village square and stopped. Beneath the glow of the street lights, their forms shivered and elongated, until two thin, skeletal forms stood side by side at the heart of the sleeping village. Seemingly from nowhere, one of the Dhouls produced a black iron rod, which it raised above its head. With one swift motion, the Dhoul plunged the rod into the cobbles of the square. A metallic clang shivered through the air and reverberated through the earth.

The two dark creatures squatted down at either side of the metal spike, grasping it with both hands, heads bowed. The one who had wielded the rod began to chant. Harsh syllables hissed through the night air, echoing off the blank faces of buildings. The iron rod began to hum beneath their hands, pulsing to the rhythm of the chant as the creatures of the Malifex poured their power into the metal. The vibration spread, slowly at first, into the ancient cobbles of the square, then to the honey-colored stone of the nearby houses.

On into the early hours of the morning, the Dhouls attended to their work, drawing into themselves the power of the Malifex and pouring it back into the iron rod beneath their hands. A deep, subsonic growl pulsed in the bedrock of the village and through the houses.

In their beds, the villagers groaned and stirred, experiencing strange, unpleasant dreams. On a dressing table, loose coins buzzed and danced. The copper pipes of several hundred plumbing systems began to resonate and sing. The hum continued to grow, building to an unbearable whine, as if the very bones of the earth were crying out in pain, and then, just when it seemed that the ground would crack and swallow the village, the tension broke and all was silent. In their beds, the people of Corfe sighed and turned over in their sleep.

Across a moonlit field, three sleek shapes raced side by side. Leaving the rough track they had been following, they found themselves on the crest of a ridge and were suddenly standing side by side, dizzy again with the transition to human form. Below them, a sweep of hillside dropped away to the south, and there, carved into the chalk, half the size of a soccer field, was the image of a human figure seated on a horse.

"There it is," said Charly.

"No," replied Amergin, shaking his head in confusion. "No, this is not right!"

"What do you mean?" demanded Sam. "What's the problem?"

"This is the wrong figure. This is not the horse we seek."

"But we followed the right directions, didn't we?" asked Sam.

"Indeed, but this is the wrong figure. There should be a horse, graceful, unburdened by a rider. Herne lies to the north; his horse alone should lie here. This figure in the pointed hat is . . . is . . . wrong!"

"Maybe," suggested Charly, "it's been altered, over the years?"

"Perhaps, child, perhaps. The location is correct, I am

certain. But how are we to find the burying place of the helm? Everything has changed." They stood without speaking, Amergin stroking his chin.

Sam broke the silence, "You know that thing you did at Old Harry? When you brought back a time when the land bridge was still there?"

"Hmmmm? Yes, my friend?" said Amergin, still deep in thought.

"Can you do anything else like that? Perhaps take us back to when the horse was how you remember it?"

"Ahh, we cannot travel back through time, my friend; the flow of history is a one-way stream. Even restoring the memory of the land, as I did at Old Harry, was a great test of my power. I fear I would fail a greater test."

"But you've got to at least try!" snapped Sam in exasperation. "You're the wizard around here, after all!"

Amergin fixed him with a steady gaze. After a moment, he said, "Very well. I will make the attempt." With that, he turned and strode away.

"Nice job," said Charly quietly.

"What?" asked Sam. "What now?"

"You can be a real brat sometimes. He's trying his best."

Sam looked sulky. "I know, but he's supposed to be the expert."

He stole a guilty glance in the direction of the wizard. Amergin was pacing back and forth, muttering under his breath. Nothing appeared to be happening.

"And you're supposed to be the big hero," replied Charly. "Isn't it about time you started being at least a little bit heroic?"

"But that's the point: I'm not a hero," protested Sam. "I never asked for this."

Amergin was squatting now, one hand pressed against the turf, fingers spread. His brows were knotted in concentration.

"Nobody asks for the things that happen to them. Do you think I asked for my dad to walk out? You just have to deal with what comes along."

Sam stared at the crouched figure of the wizard.

"Go on," said Charly softly, "go and help him."

Sam strode over to where Amergin crouched and stood behind him for a moment, then cleared his throat. "What about the two of us together, with the power of the Tear of the Sun?"

Amergin was silent for a moment, then looked back over his shoulder with a smile. "Do you know, I think you might have an idea there? Let us try." Amergin gestured for Sam to stand facing him, then turned to Charly. "Watch closely. Our attention will be fully taken up. Sam, I will lead; you supply the power." Amergin closed his eyes and clasped hands with Sam.

Sam experienced a moment of confusion—he thought that his eyes were still open, although he was sure he had closed them. Then he realized that the scene he had so recently been looking at was being reproduced behind his closed eyelids by the power of Amergin's imagination.

Then the sky began to grow lighter. A glow appeared on the western horizon and slowly spread into the reds and oranges of sunrise. The sun gathered speed, quickly rising to the top of a blue bowl of sky, before plunging into darkness in the east. "Wait a minute," thought Sam, "that's the wrong way around. It should rise in the east." After a brief darkness, the sun rose again in the west, and this time hurtled across the sky to disappear in a flash of orange. "Time must be going backward."

Again and again, the sun arched across the sky and plunged into the east. Soon, the backward flow of days reached a frequency where day and night blurred. The scene flickered like an old black-and-white film, and the landscape began to change. The trees and bushes slowly shrank and disappeared to be replaced by fully grown specimens, which in turn dwindled and were lost. Tiny human figures were occasionally visible, speeding across the fields, but soon the passage of time was so rapid that such brief phenomena were lost.

A village off in the distance shifted its boundaries, shrinking to a huddle of cottages. Abruptly, the white horse below them seemed to unravel from head to tail and was gone. They had passed the point in history at which it had been cut into the chalk!

But there, on the hillside, was another faint shape, almost lost in the grass. It was less accurate than the later version, almost a stick figure, but with a few simple lines some ancient artist had captured the essence of a horse. A lithe shape stretched across the hillside, frozen in midgallop with its chalk mane flying in the wind. As the centuries unraveled, the outline of the horse became clearer.

Amergin clearly sensed that a key point in time was approaching. He clenched Sam's hands more tightly, and the speeding passage of days began to slow.

Like a spinning top winding down, the flicker of night and day slowed, the sun rose one final time and then ground to a halt in the heavens. Its light revealed a procession approaching from the village in the distance. A motley band of men and women were being led by a tall figure in a white robe. Sam watched as they wound up the hillside and came to a halt at the horse's head.

"Quickly!" shouted Amergin. "Join them, Charly!" Charly looked at him apprehensively, then ran toward the gathering. She slowed as she got nearer, fearing that her presence would halt whatever business was about to be enacted, but the crowd seemed oblivious to her.

She moved closer to the assembled throng, edging around the wall of backs to find a clear view of the figure in white. With the exception of their leader, the members of the crowd were a rough-looking bunch, most of them not much taller than Charly, with weather-beaten faces and matted hair. Their clothes were of coarse cloth, dyed in a range of earthy browns and greens.

Feeling more confident, she reached out to tap the shoulder of a burly man in a rough-woven brown tunic. To her astonishment, her finger went straight through his shoulder. She waved her hand back and forth but felt no resistance. The figures before her were visible but physically far away in their own time. It seemed that Amergin's power was only sufficient to make the past solid but invisible, as he had at Old Harry, or visible but intangible.

Charly walked through the bodies of the crowd until she found herself at the front of a loose circle around the man in the white robe. She saw that his lips were moving but could hear no sound. It dawned on her that the crowd was totally silent. The experience was like watching TV with the sound turned off.

Charly watched as a man brought a wooden chest and placed it at the feet of the robed man. He stooped, lifted the lid, and brought forth the Helm of Herne, lifting it up for the crowd to see. The helmet was bullet-shaped and of burnished metal, which reflected a rainbow of colors. A metal band was riveted around the rim, and another band passed over the crown from back to front to form a nose guard. Two shovel-shaped cheek guards were attached to the sides by hinges, and mounted on either side of the helmet were spreading antlers, each branching to form seven points. The figure in white turned to the right and left to display the helmet, then replaced it in the chest. He gestured for the chest to be carried to the eye of the horse, where two men with shovels began to dig in the chalky soil. When they had dug a deep enough hole, the chest was placed in the ground.

The figure in white spoke a few inaudible words, then the two men filled in the hole, clods of white chalk raining down on the lid of the chest. The crowd turned and, following the man in white, filed down the hillside.

Charly walked over to the freshly turned earth and stood watching the figures retreat. Suddenly, the landscape flickered and changed; the present day had returned. Charly looked down and saw that she was standing on featureless green turf, indistinguishable from the surrounding hillside. Amergin and Sam were running down the moonlit slope toward her.

"Did you see all that?" she gasped when they arrived. "It was amazing!"

"Yes, rather successful, I thought," replied Amergin.

"Yes, but there's only one problem," said Sam. The others looked at him blankly. "No shovels!"

Charly turned to Amergin. "He's really not getting the hang of this, is he?" she asked with a smirk.

"Oh, we are making progress," smiled Amergin. "Slowly."

"What?" Sam looked from one to the other. "What?"

Suddenly, Amergin was gone, and in his place was a large badger, which ambled to the spot where Charly was standing and began to dig.

After a moment, Charly turned to Sam. "Pretty obvious, huh?"

"Yeah, yeah, yeah," Sam sighed, then wandered off to sit on the grass and watch Amergin's progress.

In a matter of minutes, Amergin had revealed the lid of the chest, just as Charly had seen it. He returned to human form and helped Sam drag the chest out of the hole. They placed it on the grass and pried open the lid. There, inside, was the helm, its metal tarnished but otherwise unaffected by the passage of years.

"It looks . . . er . . . kinda big," Sam ventured. "Will it fit?"

"Try it," suggested Amergin. Sam lifted the helmet out of the chest and placed it on his head. It was, to his surprise, a perfect fit.

"It is a magic helmet," Charly pointed out.

"This helm will confer a considerable degree of protection against the power of the Malifex," said Amergin, "but remember—it cannot make you invulnerable. Use it with care. Now, we must return. Dawn is drawing near."

Again, they found themselves in the shape of deer, speeding across the fields as the first gray light of dawn bled into the eastern sky. They narrowly avoided being spotted by Charly's uncle as they crept into the farmyard in the early morning. He was bringing the cows in to be milked, and they were forced to revert to their human forms and hide behind a stone wall until he had passed. As the cattle filed off toward the outbuildings, Charly's uncle stopped and looked around, as if some sound or smell had caught his attention, before following his charges. Sam, Charly, and Amergin crept into the cottage, footsore and exhausted, and were soon asleep.

chapter 11

Later that morning, Megan peeped into Charly's bedroom, but she was still sleeping, so she closed the door quietly and went about her business. She had no intention of disturbing Mr. Wisdom in his room, which was fortunate, as she would have found Sam fast asleep in a sleeping bag on the floor. Around midmorning, there was a caller at the door, but the sounds of knocking and subsequent conversation failed to wake the three sleepers.

Megan sat at the kitchen table, deep in thought. The dark-haired visitor in the stylish suit was long gone, but his visit had left her with a feeling of deep unease. She tried to put her finger on what was wrong. The man had been charming in an old-fashioned way, but something about him disturbed her. Then it came to her; he had no aura. In all her life, she had never come across anyone who lacked an aura. Sometimes they were very difficult to see, but she had become adept at spotting them over the years. Perhaps, somehow, he was suppressing it? But what sort of person would have the power, and the need, to suppress their own aura?

In addition to her concerns about the visit of the strange man, Megan was far from happy about Mr.

Wisdom, if that was his real name. Even her own daughter was acting strangely. "Always listen to your instincts," her mother used to say, and her mother had been a wise woman.

She wandered around the kitchen, humming to herself, waiting for the tea kettle to boil, but the feeling of unease remained. "Oh, well," she sighed, "only one thing for it." She made herself a mug of chamomile tea, collected a few items from various cupboards, and headed for her study. Locking the door behind her, Megan went over to a bookcase in a corner of the room and pulled out an old notebook. Handling it with a strange reverence, she took it over to the desk, where she settled down to read.

The book, old and tattered with a faded brown paper cover, was her *Book of Lights and Shadows*. Most witches had one, given to them by the person who first introduced them to the Craft. Megan was given hers by her mother, and it contained a lifetime of wisdom. The idea of the book was to write down everything that you thought might be of use to future practitioners of the Craft, every charm and spell you had tried, every herbal remedy, thought, idea, ritual. In this way, the Wiccan tradition was passed on from generation to generation. Some books, particularly those belonging to a certain kind of modern witch, were terribly serious, full of stern rituals and bad poetry. Megan was rather old-fashioned in this respect and disapproved of anyone who thought that Wicca involved wearing occult jewelery and too much eye makeup.

Her *Book of Lights and Shadows* was very much a practical document. It had grown in an organic way as it was passed down the generations and was full of pressed flowers, baby photographs, and old shopping lists, as well as charms and cures. As a result, it was always difficult to find a particular piece of information.

Absentmindedly, Megan rose and wandered over to her favorite armchair, where she curled up and continued to browse. She had a catlike way of moving that came from being completely comfortable with herself. Charly was beginning to show signs of this, but she had also inherited some of her father's nervous energy, as well as his sharp tongue.

Megan flicked through the pages, pausing to read a long-forgotten recipe for drop scones, before finding the page she was looking for and settling down to read more intently.

After ten minutes or so, Megan jumped to her feet and began to bustle around the study. First, she drew the curtains, then began to clear a space on the floor, which was still strewn with books. She gathered together the things she had brought with her from the kitchen, adding other items that she retrieved from around the room. Her tidying exposed an old rug, containing a circular design in rich purples and reds, on which she began to arrange the items according to some familiar pattern.

Megan placed four candlesticks at equal distances around the circle in the rug's central design. The candles were at the four main compass points: north, south, east, and west. Using her left hand, she placed the eastern candle first, then worked clockwise to the south, west, and north.

By the eastern candle, she placed a smoldering stick of incense in a long wooden holder. The rising smoke symbolized the element of air. Next to the southern candle, she placed a tiny oil lamp made of polished brass with a glass shade to represent fire. Then came the items she had brought from the kitchen. She put a cup of water by the western candle and a bowl of salt, symbolizing earth, to the north. Once the four elements—earth, air, fire, and water—were present, Megan took a pinch of salt, sprinkled it in the cup of water with a muttered invocation, then settled down cross-legged in the center of the circle, breathing deeply.

When calm and centered enough to continue, she rose and took from her pocket a black-handled knife with a polished silver blade, engraved with strange symbols. She had bought this knife—or athame—many years ago. It had been very expensive, but, as with all her magical tools, she had never questioned the cost. Strangely, though, the athame was never used for cutting, at least not in the physical sense, but only as a kind of pointer in rituals.

Facing north, Megan began the ritual with the following words:

> I conjure thee, O Circle of Power, to be a
> shield against all wickedness and evil, to
> preserve and contain the Power that I raise
> within thee. I bless and consecrate thee in
> the names of Aradia and Cernunnos.

Turning to the east, she raised the athame and said, "Lords of the Watchtowers of the East, Lords of Air, I do summon you and call you up . . . " and so on, around the circle, at each point invoking the lords of the appropriate element.

As she did this, she imagined a circle of light trailing from the tip of her outthrust dagger so that, at the end of the invocation, she was enclosed in a glowing sphere. Finally, she threw out her arms and said:

> I surround myself with the pure
> white light of the Goddess.
> Good shall come to me,
> I give thanks to she who bore me.

Thus protected from evil influences, Megan began the task she had set herself. Her *Book of Lights and Shadows* contained a bewildering range of spells and charms for all needs and occasions, but most of them had one purpose— to focus the mind on the job at hand. Many of the more recent ones were terribly serious, drawing on Greek and Norse mythology, but Megan preferred to begin with an old rhyme called "The Witches' Rune." It belonged to what she thought of as the Black Hats and Broomsticks school of witchcraft, and she found she could never take herself too seriously when she used it. Right now, she felt as if she needed cheering up.

"Darksome night and shining Moon," she began, arms crossed over her chest.

> East, then South, then West, then North.
> Harken to the Witches' Rune.
> Here come I to call Thee forth.
> By all the powers of land and sea,
> Wand and pentacle and sword
> Be obedient to me.

Harken ye unto my word.
Scourge and censer, cords and knife,
Powers of the Witches' Blade,
Harken ye all unto life.
Come ye as the charm is made.
Queen of Heaven, Queen of Hell,
Queen of Earth, and sea, and night.
Send Thy aid unto the spell.
Work my spell by magick rite.
By all the powers of land and sea,
By all the might of moon and sun,
As I do say so mote it be—
Chant the spell and it be done.

With that, she again settled down cross-legged in the center of the rug, picked up a deck of tarot cards, and began to place them before her. She studied them for a while, then scooped them up, shuffled them, and carefully dealt them out once more. For more than half an hour, she repeated this process, far longer than for a normal reading, but then she had never seen the cards turn out like this before.

Certain patterns kept repeating; the Four of Swords, in particular, seemed significant. The card depicted a figure—a knight in armor—lying on a stone slab, as if in a tomb. It was generally held to represent vigilance and solitude, perhaps exile, and it kept turning up with the Hanged Man, meaning wisdom or prophecy. The High Priestess, which could signify a man as easily as a woman, again suggested wisdom but also the mysteries of the future, as yet unrevealed.

In opposition to all this was a force represented by the King of Cups, a severe figure holding a scepter and a golden goblet, seated on a throne in the middle of the sea. The card was upside down, or reversed, which gave it the meaning of a dishonest man. The King of Swords was also reversed, meaning cruelty or evil intention, and it appeared with Strength, again reversed, representing abuse of power, and the Tower, signifying ruin and misery.

There seemed to be a third strand to her reading, a minor thread, but growing in significance the more she pursued it. The Page of Pentacles depicted a boy holding aloft a five-pointed star and had the meaning of study or learning. Several times it turned up alongside the Three of Pentacles, which signified someone of skill but also someone destined for glory. Associated with these cards were the Wheel of Fortune, meaning destiny, and the Moon, suggesting hidden enemies, danger, darkness, and terror.

Megan turned over one last card. A grotesque, red figure with the horns of a goat and the wings of a huge bat stared back at her— the Devil. At his feet were two lesser demons, chained to a pillar, and in his hand was a flaming torch. The Devil was a confusing card. It had the obvious meanings of violence and destruction but also signified something that was destined to be but was not necessarily evil.

Megan scooped up the cards, put them back in their packet, and stood up. With a sigh, she pulled out her athame, cut the circle of light, and began to tidy up the study.

Ten minutes later, Megan let herself out of the back door of the cottage, glancing left and right, and moved purposefully around her small garden with a wicker basket and a pair of old kitchen scissors. Returning to the house, she began to hang up sprigs of fennel, mugwort, and vervain over the doors and windows. Then she returned to the kitchen table and sat, head bowed, waiting for her daughter to wake.

The herbs she had picked and hung around the house were all regarded as potent protectors against evil. Megan hoped they would be enough.

Just before midday, Charly emerged, bleary-eyed, from her room.

"Ah, there you are," said her mother when Charly finally wandered into the kitchen in search of food. "I thought you were going to sleep all day. I suppose while you're on vacation you might as well make the most of it." Charly mumbled something about not getting to sleep until late and rummaged in the fridge. "I haven't seen Mr. Wisdom today either. I suppose he might have gone out early. He had a visitor this morning, a man in a fancy suit. There was something ... I don't know ... creepy about him. You know how I get these feelings sometimes!" Charly nodded. "Anyway, I sent him on his way, told him Norman—Mr. Wisdom, I should say—was out."

"Did he say who he was or what he wanted?" Charly asked.

"Well, only that he wanted to speak to Mr. Wisdom— actually, he didn't mention his name, come to think of it. He just said, "You have someone staying with you. I have a message for him." It really gave me the creeps. He said his name was . . . what was it? . . . oh yes . . . Halifax. Mr. Halifax." Charly looked up from her sandwich with a start. "Anyway, I'm going into town after lunch," continued her mother. "Want to come, too?"

"Er . . . yes. Maybe. I'll . . . er . . . let you know later." Charly picked up her sandwich and the various other bits of food she had collected when her mother was looking elsewhere and ran off to find Sam and Amergin.

Knocking briefly on the bedroom door, she burst in and hissed, "Wake up, you two. Trouble!" She threw various packets of munchies onto the bed and Sam's sleeping bag, then flung herself into a chair in the corner. "The Malifex has been here this morning, looking for one of you, not sure which one. Mom didn't let him in—said you were out," she looked at Amergin, "but I doubt he believed her."

"Then we should be on our way as soon as possible," said Amergin. "Our next target should be the Spear of Destiny."

"Where do we find that?" asked Sam.

"Ah, the spear lies beneath the Puckstone," Amergin replied.

"Okay," said Sam patiently, "and where's that?"

Charly piped up, "It's not far from the Agglestone."

"Great. Thanks," Sam sighed. "That's completely cleared that up."

"Out toward the ferry at Sandbanks," explained Charly. "Not easy to get to, but I think I can find it. I've been to the Agglestone with Granddad. Mom said she was going into town later. We could get a lift part of the way with her."

"Excellent," replied Amergin. "Let us prepare."

"I'll come and get you when we're ready to go." And with that, Charly bustled off to find her mother.

Three-quarters of an hour later, they were ready to depart. Charly's mother sold some of her pottery to a small craft shop in Corfe and had loaded the trunk with her most recent creations. Charly brought Sam and Amergin, having explained to her mother that the three of them were going to look at the castle for the afternoon and would make their own way back by bus. As they were about to get into the car, Charly's Uncle Pete came striding across the farmyard toward them.

"Hi, Pete," said Charly's mom. "Just going to Corfe. Anything you need?"

"No thanks, Megan. The missus went into Wareham yesterday. This must be your guest," he said looking squarely at Amergin.

"Wisdom," said Amergin, shaking his hand.

"And you're the lad staying at the cottage?" Uncle Pete turned to Sam. A gruff voice sounded in Sam's head. "You shall not prevail. The agents of the Malifex are all around you. Leave while you still may." Sam looked up into Uncle Pete's eyes, where a bright green light flared and was gone.

"Come on then, folks, let's get going," said Charly's mom, climbing into the car. "See you later, Pete."

Sam hurried into the back seat of the car next to Amergin. Charly climbed into the front next to her mother. Once the engine had rumbled into life and they were pulling away, Sam whispered to Amergin, "Did you hear that?"

"I heard, my friend. The Malifex will be closing in. We should expect this in light of our success to date, but we must be on our guard."

They helped Charly's mother unload her pottery from the back of the car, then headed toward the castle. The village was busy. It was a sunny afternoon, and crowds of tourists were evident. The three of them loitered outside the entrance to the castle, waiting until Charly's mother headed for home. After a minute, Amergin reached out and took Sam and Charly by the shoulder. "Stay close," he said, "something is wrong." He nodded across the square. At first, Sam could see nothing unusual. Then he noticed that here and there in the crowd of tourists and daily shoppers, the occasional figure had stopped and was looking across at them. All around the village, square eyes were fixed in their direction. "I think," Amergin continued, "we may be in trouble."

The three of them stood closer together, glancing nervously around the square. A number of people started to move toward them, workers, middle-aged ladies, tourists— all converged purposefully toward the castle entrance. Then Charly spotted two tall figures in dark suits and sunglasses at the top of the square.

"Look!" she pointed. "Our friends are back."

Amergin turned to her. "How were you planning to get to the Puckstone?"

"By bus," replied Charly, "the same one we caught before.

It goes from down there." She pointed to where the main road ran through the village.

"And how long must we wait?"

Charly glanced at her watch. "About fifteen minutes," she said reluctantly.

"I fear," replied Amergin, "that we do not have fifteen minutes. However, I think we should get moving."

They set off at a brisk walk, dodging through the knots of tourists, but all around them determined figures were closing in. In front of them, the pavement was blocked by two burly men in fluorescent yellow vests and hard hats. Sam saw a glint of green in their eyes. He pulled at Amergin's sleeve, directing him between two parked cars. Charly followed close behind as they made their way down the road. A family—mother and father with two young children—was angling across the road to intercept them, forcing them to duck back onto the pavement.

Suddenly, an elderly gentleman, emerald eyes blazing, stepped out of a shop doorway and grabbed Charly by the arm. She lashed out with her foot, catching him on the shin, and shouted "Run!" She twisted free of his grasp and ran down the road, hard on the heels of Sam and Amergin. "Head around to the left," she called after them. "Then we'll at least be on the bus route, in case it turns up."

All around the village center, people broke into a run behind them. The bottom end of the square, down toward the main road, was relatively free of people, and it looked as if their escape route was clear. They turned the corner onto the main road and hurtled around the base of the castle. They had a good lead over their pursuers, but Amergin in particular was growing short of breath. Rounding another corner, Amergin came to an abrupt halt. Up ahead was a public parking lot full of cars and buses. They saw a mob of people running toward them. They looked around frantically for a way of escape. To their left was the high perimeter wall of the castle. Amergin gestured for them to cross the road, where there was a row of cottages. There seemed to be no prospect of escape there either, but it was somehow less daunting than the high castle wall. They jogged along looking desperately for some way out.

Sam stopped, panting, with his hands on his knees. There seemed no point in running any more. He noticed, with a kind of detachment, that the wall next to him had huge spiral fossils cemented into it. They somehow added to the sense of unreality. "Maybe this is just a nightmare," he thought. "Maybe I'll wake up soon." Both behind and in front of them, the green-eyed mobs were closing in.

chapter 12

Just as Sam had given up hope, a car screeched to a halt opposite them and the voice of Charly's mom shouted, "Don't just stand there! Get in!"

The three of them tumbled gratefully into the car as Charly's mother put her foot to the floor and sped off, with a screech of tires, past the contorted faces of the pursuing crowd. A bunch of herbs, hanging from the rear-view mirror, swung wildly back and forth as the car swerved past the approaching throng. Sam had a jumbled impression of gaping mouths and green eyes as they broke through the thickest part of the mob. Frustrated hands slapped against the car windows, and a few people ran after them but were soon left behind.

Just outside the village, when the danger seemed to have passed and their speed had dropped back to something less breathtaking, Charly's mother said, "All right, one of you had better explain what's going on."

Sam, Amergin, and Charly looked at each other sheepishly, none of them wishing to be the first to speak. Charly's mom broke the silence for them. "I may come across as scatterbrained, but don't ever assume that I'm stupid. Oh, you've all done very well, with your stories and excuses, but you're fooling nobody. First of all," she glanced at Charly," Mr. Wisdom turns up out of the blue, with some half-baked story about being a local historian. Well, he knows precious little about the local area and more about ancient history than anyone has a right to, unless they were there." She stared pointedly in the mirror. "And then there's the way you speak, Mr. Wisdom—or whatever your real name is. Very convincing until you get excited, and then . . . well, it's unusual, to say the least. So, the three of you go traipsing around the countryside, and I'm supposed to believe that you're sightseeing." She shook her head. "But the final straw was Pete."

The other three remained silent. "I may not be an expert in the Craft, unlike some," she glanced at Amergin again, "but I'm not entirely without skill. I could tell there was something wrong with Uncle Pete. His aura was wrong. He was radiating pain, as if he was being made to do something against his will. And you," now she looked at Sam in the mirror, "you looked as if you'd seen a ghost after he spoke to you. So I hung around in Corfe to see what you were up to. Looking around the castle! You must think I was born yesterday! Lucky for you I wasn't. No, I consulted the cards this morning, and they told me a lot. Something bad is happening, something evil, and you, Mr. Wisdom, are at the heart of it. The Four of Swords, a man of wisdom, vigilant, waiting in exile. And you," she looked to Sam, "are the apprentice, the Page of Pentacles, destined for glory. So, who's the third? The man with no aura who turned up on my doorstep, the King of Swords reversed?"

So, with Charly taking the lead and the others joining in with explanations and comments, they told her all that had happened in the last few days.

" . . . and then after Sam had turned me into a hamster," Megan glanced at Sam in the mirror, Sam shrugged, "we found Herne's horse, only it was the wrong horse, so Amergin turned back time, and I watched where the wizard buried the helm, and then Amergin turned into a badger and dug it up, and then we turned back into deer and came home, but then the Malifex—that was the man at the door—must have come while we were asleep, and now Uncle Pete's one of them like all those people in Corfe, and I'm so glad you turned up, Mom," Charly finished breathlessly.

"Well," Charly's mom turned to the back seat, "you should be ashamed of yourself, Amergin, or whatever your name is. Getting kids mixed up in a business like this."

"Madam, I assure you . . . " began Amergin, but Charly's mom was full of righteous indignation.

"And having gotten them into this mess, you should certainly have come to me for help. As I say, I am not without skill."

"I am sure that is the case, madam,"

"Oh, spare me the madam routine. My name's Megan."

"Yes . . . er . . . Megan, but you must understand, I am millennia adrift from my own time. I must make my way as best I can. I was told a great hero would awaken me, and I expected to be able to draw on the wisdom of the great sorcerers and druids of this time. Instead . . . " He gestured around him forlornly.

"Hmmmm," conceded Megan grudgingly, "I suppose you were only doing what you thought best. Men! Honestly, you'd all rather drive around lost for hours than stop and ask for directions."

"So, what are you going to do now, Mom?" asked Charly.

"Do? What do you think I'm going to do? Let's go and find this spear!"

Charly and Sam exchanged a smile of relief.

"Do you know anything about the Puckstone?" asked Amergin.

"Not much," admitted Megan. "I visited the Agglestone with my father but not the Puckstone. Puck, of course, is another name for the Green Man."

Sam looked blank. For his benefit, Megan explained, "He's an archetypal figure from pre-Christian mythology."

Amergin continued, "A figure from the earliest human legends, associated with rebirth and the turning wheel of the seasons. You remember I told you that the Malifex was the personification of evil, a human face given to the natural forces of destruction and death?" Sam nodded. "Well, the forces of birth, of life and creation also have a face— the Green Man, Puck, Jack-in-the-Green. He has had many names and has haunted the fringes of human knowledge for millennia, a leafy face in the wild woods. However, unlike the Malifex, he shuns human contact."

"Shouldn't he be fighting the Malifex, rather than us?" asked Charly.

"A perceptive question," agreed Amergin, "and one that has troubled the wisest of the wise. The Green Man would be a powerful ally indeed, and, in the past when the dark tide has threatened, a few brave souls have gone to seek his aid. Some never returned. Of those who did, most had wandered in the wild until they lost their wits. Others came back mad with terror. The Green Man, if indeed he exists, is a natural force, like the wind and the sea. You do not enlist the aid of the sea. It follows its own path."

"And you think this stone was named after him?" asked Megan.

"Who can tell?" replied Amergin. "Come. We should be on our way."

Megan had driven through the village of Studland and turned down a rough track that wound off to their left. She brought the car to a halt, and the four of them walked to the end of the lane, where a footpath struck off in the general direction of the Puckstone. As soon as they were out of sight, a long black car with darkened windows pulled into the lane behind them, tires crunching on the gravel.

With Megan leading and Amergin bringing up the rear, they emerged onto a vast expanse of rolling heathland and followed a sandy path through gorse and heather, which scratched at their legs and caught hold of their clothing. A cold wind with a hint of rain behind it sighed through the low bushes, and gray clouds scudded overhead.

"That's the Agglestone, over there." Megan pointed to their left, where a massive block of stone was silhouetted against the skyline. "The Puckstone should be straight ahead."

The path branched several times. After some consultation, they decided to ignore it and headed in a straight line for where Megan thought the stone should be. The ground became damper, until they found themselves in an expanse of peat bog, covered in bright green moss and streams and pools of black water. The sodden ground sucked at their feet. Sam stumbled and fell.

"Hey!" he exclaimed. "The ground moved!"

"The peat moss acts like a huge sponge," explained Megan. "It fills up old lakes and forms a skin over the top. If you jump up and down, you'll see the whole thing start to wobble. Just make sure you don't fall through."

Sam looked at the ground with suspicion as he clambered to his feet and moved on. They picked their way cautiously through a maze of pools and channels, trying to step on the drier tussocks of sedge and heather. Eventually, the ground began to rise again, and, standing on the drier ground, Megan said, "There it is." Ahead, they could see a massive dark boulder, smaller than the Agglestone but still imposing as it rose from the rolling landscape of the heath. Leaving the path once more, they made their way more quickly toward their destination.

Upon reaching it, Charly saw that the boulder rested on a natural plinth of underlying rock, as if it had been deposited there by a giant's hand.

"So," said Sam, "you think the spearhead is underneath that?"

"So I am led to believe," agreed Amergin.

"And how do you suggest we get at it?"

"We will have to lift the stone, obviously." Amergin looked at him impatiently. "Come—time is growing short. I feel danger is approaching." He instructed Sam to stand facing the rock, then he himself moved to a point about a third of the way around from Sam. "Madam ... er ... Megan? Would you care to assist?"

"Just try and stop me," replied Charly's mother with grim determination. Amergin gestured for her to stand on the far side of the stone, so that the three of them formed a triangle.

"Charly," said Amergin, "stand wherever you wish, but be ready to run in and get the spearhead when I give the word. Now—Sam, Megan—close your eyes and lend me your strength. Do you have the Tear of the Sun?" Sam pulled the pendant from within his shirt. "Then we will begin."

Sam closed his eyes and felt Amergin reach out to his mind. He could see the Puckstone in front of him, could sense its massive mineral bulk. He could almost see inside, into the complex layers and planes, and taste the crisp tingle of the crystals that made up the rock. Energy began to flow from him, Megan, and the Tear of the Sun and was channeled into the rock. Its crystal structure resonated to an energy frequency dictated by Amergin. Slowly, the flow of power increased until the stone seemed to pulsate, and then, in his imagination, Sam saw the Puckstone begin to rise.

With a wrench, it left behind the table of rock upon which it had rested for millennia and, wobbling slightly, rose a few inches into the air. Amergin increased his demand for energy. Sam felt the drain as a cold sensation in his extremities and had a sudden desire to sleep. The Tear of the Sun throbbed against his chest.

The Puckstone was about a hand's width above the ground. Sam could just make out the edges of a shallow depression where the stone had rested. He braced himself as the power drain increased yet again. His arms and legs were starting to go numb, and he was desperately sleepy. Only the pounding in his head kept him focused.

When the stone was about three feet off the ground, Amergin shouted, "Charly! Now!"

Charly darted in, flung herself full length on the ground, and thrust one hand under the stone. Then she rolled back on to the surrounding grass, clutching a small bundle, just as the Puckstone crashed back into place with a hollow boom and a cloud of dust.

Sam, Amergin, and Megan rushed over to where Charly was sitting. Sam felt extremely light-headed, and Megan had gone very pale.

"Go on," said Sam impatiently, "open it!"

Charly carefully unwrapped the bundle, which seemed to be made of a cross between thick paper and thin leather and was stiff with grease. Inside was a silver spearhead, slightly longer than Sam's hand, delicately engraved in a style similar to the Tear of the Sun, with a round socket for a spearshaft at one end.

Sam looked up at Amergin. "We did it!" he exclaimed.

From behind the Puckstone came the sound of clapping hands. "Oh, bravo," said a deep voice, as the Malifex emerged from behind the rock. "Awfully good of you! That looked like hard work." Behind him stood two impassive dark figures. "And now you will hand the spearhead over to me." The Malifex held out his hand.

"Get behind me," Amergin hissed, rising to his feet. He held the package containing the spearhead in one hand. "Spirit of Darkness," Amergin called out, "if you desire the spear, then you will have to take it from me."

"Do you know," asked the Malifex with a tight smile, "I was rather hoping you would say that." He raised one hand, index finger pointed at Amergin. There was a shimmer in the air around him, and a flash of darkness crackled from his outstretched finger toward Amergin.

Amergin intercepted the bolt with one upraised palm and stood, feet braced, as a wall of dark energy, veined with blue lightning, crackled in front of him. The wall of evil force gradually shrank and disappeared.

"Very good!" exclaimed the Malifex. "But not, I fear, good enough. You have been awake long enough now to see something of this world. Surely you realize that my dominion is nearly complete? Look around you, fool! The old magic is gone, forgotten! I have brought the world something better, something people want more. I have brought them a kind of blind, stupid happiness, with their televisions, cars, and cell phones. And the beauty of it is, I hardly had to try! Every idea I whispered down the ages was seized upon with glee! Eight-lane highways? Absolutely! Pesticides in food and water? Why not? Factories belching poison into the air? Yes, please!

"People that stupid, my friend, deserve to be dominated. Which is just what I intend to do, once I have relieved you of that little trinket." As he had been speaking, the Dhouls had moved to stand closer, and now each reached out and placed a hand on the shoulder of the Malifex.

He raised both his hands, fingers outstretched, and closed his eyes. As he muttered under his breath, the air around him became icy. White vapor dripped from his arms and crawled across the ground. Suddenly, his eyes snapped open, blazing green. There was a vast black detonation, and a ripple passed through the earth beneath their feet. Amergin was flung backward, colliding with Megan and Charly. The three of them fell to the ground. Sam rushed to their side. The Malifex stretched out and caught the spearhead as it flew from Amergin's grasp.

"And so we part, my young friend," the Malifex said to Sam as he slipped the spearhead into the inside pocket of his jacket. "If it is any consolation at all, you came out of this better than your predecessor, Arthur. He may have won, but I understand he was in no condition to enjoy his victory. Be thankful you are still alive." He turned and, flanked by his two servants, marched across the heath.

Sam turned to Megan, who was cradling Amergin's head in her lap. "Is he . . . ?" Sam began.

"He's still alive," replied Megan, "but only just. His breathing is very shallow."

Amergin moaned, his head rolling from side to side. His eyes flickered open. "Sam," he whispered, "come closer." Sam knelt down by his side. "One . . . last chance," muttered Amergin and reached out to Sam. He placed his fingertips on Sam's forehead for a moment, then slumped back into unconsciousness.

"No," said Sam, a look of horror on his face. "No! You said . . . ! Amergin, I can't!"

"What is it?" asked Charly in concern.

"Leave me alone!" snapped Sam. "Leave me alone," he repeated, more quietly. "I just ... need a minute." He scrambled to his feet and walked to the far side of the Puckstone, where he sat on the ground with his back against the rock.

This wasn't funny any more, he thought to himself. At first, it had all been pretty exciting, a refreshing change from the usual family vacation. Then the Malifex had cast some sort of spell on his parents and Uncle Pete, and it had all stopped being a game. Now it came down to him. He was on his own, without guidance, with no real idea of how to use the powers he seemed to possess and with a terrifying choice in front of him. Sensibly, he should do what the Malifex said—be thankful he wasn't lying there like Amergin. Forget it all, go home ... but he couldn't go home, could he? His parents, as far as he knew, were still sitting, frozen, at the cottage breakfast table.

Even if the Malifex had released them or the spell wore off, which he doubted, what could he do? Go back to school? Move on with the rest of his life, always knowing that there was a point where he might have made a difference? A point where it all came down to him, and that everything that happened thereafter, all the bad things in the world, were his fault? Suddenly, he hated the Malifex, hated him with a bitter intensity, not just for what he had done to the world, not even for what he had done to his parents and Charly's uncle, but for making him responsible for it all.

He jumped to his feet and marched back to where Charly and her mother were still tending to Amergin's motionless body. "Can you do anything for him?" he asked Megan with new strength in his voice.

"I might be able to, but all my herbs are at home."

"Come on, then," said Sam. "Let's get him home."

They half-dragged, half-carried Amergin back to the car, Sam bolstering their strength with the Tear of the Sun, which he clasped in one hand. They drove back in silence and pulled into the farmyard as dusk was falling. After they had bundled Amergin into the cottage, Sam left him in the care of Charly and her mother and went to the room he had shared with the wizard. He sat on the bed for a while, staring into space, then rose, left the house, and walked across the yard to his family's cottage. A few minutes later, Charly saw him return and disappear into the bedroom once more.

There, he took out the Helm of Herne from its hiding place and laid it on the bed next to the Tear of the Sun. "Two power-ups out of a possible three," he thought to himself. "Well, I've finished games in worse shape than that before."

There was a knock on the door, and Charly came in and sat on the bed next to him. "You're going somewhere, aren't you?" she asked.

"Yes. I'm going to finish this," he replied. "I've just been over to our cottage," he continued. "My parents, they're still there. The way he left them. That kind of settles it."

"So what are you going to do? What did Amergin say to you?"

Sam turned and looked her in the eyes.

"He told me to go and find the Green Man."

chapter 13

"But, Amergin said . . . " began Charly. "You can't! He said that the Green Man never helps. That people who go looking come back crazy. Or . . . or don't come back at all!"

"So what do I do?" Sam demanded. "I can't just leave Mom and Dad there like that. I can't let him win, don't you understand that?"

"Okay, fair enough, but I'm coming with you."

"Oh, no! No, you're not. It's bad enough that I have to go. You stay here with Amergin."

"Amergin will be fine with Mom. He's asleep now. You need me, Sam. You're not a hero. You need my help—I know stuff, I can give you advice. You don't even know where to look!"

"But I do," replied Sam. Charly looked at him in surprise. "It's all in my head," he explained, tapping one temple with his finger. "Amergin put it there. Everything I need to know. It's all there if I look for it."

Charly sighed. "Sam, look. This is difficult. I . . . well, I'm part of all this now. I was there from the start. I crossed the invisible bridge to Old Harry. I stood on top of Maiden Castle with you, with all the ley lines lit up. You can't ask me to just stop. You owe it to me. And anyway," she looked down at the floor, "I'll be terrified if I have to sit around here just waiting for you to come back."

Sam looked rueful. "Even worse. If I come back in one piece, and I've seen the Green Man, you'll make my life miserable." He smiled at her. "Looks like we're a team, but you can't tell your mother."

"I think," said Charly, nodding, "that it might be better if we didn't mention this."

Later that night, after Charly's mother had fallen asleep on a camp bed next to Amergin, they met outside the cottage. Sam had the Tear of the Sun around his neck and, when Charly was ready, he placed the Helm of Herne on his head. Charly began to giggle, stuffing her gloved hand in her mouth.

"What?" asked Sam with a sigh.

"The tennis shoes sort of ruin the effect," she gasped in a hoarse whisper.

Sam looked down at his feet. "King Arthur wore tennis shoes, trust me." He managed a smile, but both of them were dreading having to make a move, to set off into the unknown.

"So," asked Charly briskly, "where are we off to? I'll be your local guide."

"I don't think so. Not this time," Sam replied. "We're going to Dartmoor."

"Dartmoor!" Charly exploded. "That's miles!"

"More than a hundred miles as the crow flies," Sam confirmed.

"So how were you planning on getting there?"

"Ah, smarty, losing your touch?" Sam smiled again. "As

the crow flies?" There was a flash, and, in a flurry of wings, two black crows took to the air, wheeled once over the farm, and set off to the west.

Sam sighted down his straight, black beak, reading the wind. The instructions Amergin had given him were all there in his head like some strange map. Instead of roads, the landscape was mapped out in lines and swirls of magnetic force, patterns of stars and shifting winds, and the faint but ever-increasing taste of the sea.

By his side, Charly reveled in the feel of the wind beneath her wings, her individual primary feathers flexing and tensing as she slid down a hill of air, her senses filled with the language of the wind and the faint heat from villages and towns far below. Side by side, they flew on through the night as the moon rose and fell. Sometime after midnight, they stopped to rest in the top of a tall tree, panting in the swaying branches. A bewildering flow of nighttime noises shifted around them. Roosting starlings, disturbed by their unusual nocturnal visitors, started to wake with increasing clamor. All too soon, Sam took to the air again, and Charly was forced to follow.

Toward dawn, the land began to rise, became wilder and more rugged. The villages thinned out and were gone. They were over Dartmoor. As the first gray light of the sun spread into the sky, Sam circled over a desolate expanse of high moorland, then dropped like an arrow toward a patch of forest.

Charly fluttered to a halt beside him on an outcrop of lichen-crusted rock, and, in the blink of an eye, they were standing in human form.

"Well," said Sam, breathless and apprehensive, "if Amergin's right, this is the place."

"Then I suppose," Charly replied, "we should go in."

They walked up a slope of bleached grass and scattered boulders. As the wood grew nearer, they were surprised to see the trees were only slightly taller than head height. They were ancient and gnarled oaks, their branches twisted against the lightening sky like tortured limbs. Everywhere, moss and lichen dripped from the branches in the damp, still air. Sam and Charly paused on the threshold, glanced at each other, then stepped inside.

After a few paces, the sound of the wind had died away, and they were lost in a strange, tumbled world of mossy boulders and the contorted forms of ancient trees. The instructions Amergin had given Sam ran out here, so they stumbled toward the heart of the wood, as they remembered it from the air.

The ground was so uneven that they were forced to scramble on all fours and were soon covered in green stains. The Helm of Herne was knocked from Sam's head several times, and he had to stop to retrieve it from fern-filled crevices. At last they came to a clearing, where there was a rough circle of boulders. Charly sat down on one of the stones. Sam walked into the center and looked around. The wood was silent; not even birdsong could be heard. He wandered back and forth, then stopped and shouted, "Hello!"

His voice fell flat. He adjusted the helmet on his head and took the Tear of the Sun from inside his shirt, fiddling with it as he walked backward and forward.

"An interesting bauble," said a voice from behind him. The voice was rich and musical, as if several voices were speaking at once and bells were ringing in the background. Sam spun around. A tall figure was advancing from the darkness between the trees. It was somehow difficult to figure out the details because the darkness seemed to follow him, but he appeared to be a tall, broad-shouldered figure with the voice of a man. Leaves issued from his mouth and twined into a mane of hair, which resembled foliage. A pair of large amber eyes peered from under leafy brows. The face seemed vaguely familiar. Then Sam remembered the ceramic face on the wall of Charly's cottage and the pictures on the walls of her mother's study.

"Explain, child," said the voice, "what brings you here, and why do you have such a toy?"

Sam glanced over at Charly and saw, with a chill of fear, that she had slumped to the floor.

"She is unharmed," said the figure. "She is of the Goddess and therefore beyond my power to harm. She merely sleeps. Now . . . explain."

"Er . . . I . . . " Sam began. "Are you the Green Man?" It seemed a pointless question under the circumstances.

"I have had many names," replied the figure, "but that has been one of them."

"I was sent to ask for your help. The Malifex . . . "

"Ah, the same reason. Always the same reason. Were you not told, child? I do not involve myself in the affairs of humankind."

"Why not?" demanded Sam. "You should! This is your business, not mine!"

The Green Man raised a hand in Sam's direction, and the amber eyes flared, sparks of golden light in the gloom. Sam felt a prickling on his skin, a crawling sensation. Suddenly, something was slithering up his legs, over his chest, beneath his clothes. He could feel a brush of leaves, the rough touch of bark as if vines or creepers were writhing around him. Something burst out of the collar of his shirt and wrapped itself around his face, pushing against his mouth. Tendrils forced themselves into his nose and ears, fine rootlets bristling and scratching. His mouth was filled with the acrid taste of soil, old leaf mold, decay. He clutched at his face, trying to rip away the strangling vines, but there was nothing beneath his fingers. He grasped the Tear of the Sun and concentrated on the truth: that the sensations were illusion. Slowly, the choking feeling receded. Sam opened his eyes and stared defiantly at the Green Man.

"You are bolder than many who have sought me out, child. For that, I will try to explain. Sit." The Green Man gestured to a rock. He appeared to sit cross-legged at the edge of the stone circle, although it was hard to tell. The darkness seemed to draw around him like a cloak, and he became a rough, organic shape, part of the landscape.

"What do you see, when you look at me?" asked the Green Man.

"Well, it's difficult," said Sam. "I can't seem to look at you. My eyes sort of wander off, but you look humanish. Tall, green hair, brown eyes."

"The fox sees me otherwise," rumbled the figure, "and the deer, otherwise again. Each sees only what he or she may understand, but none of these forms is true, and none of them is false."

Sam looked blank.

"Let me tell you a tale, child. Long ago, twelve thousand years as you would measure it, the world was cold. Ice covered this land. Then, slowly, the world grew warmer, and the ice began to retreat northward, leaving behind a land of bare earth and rock, carved into new shapes by the weight of the ice. As the ice retreated, a few hardy plants followed from the warmer south—Britain was not an island in those days, you must understand—and slowly the land became green again. Then the trees came, marching in from the European continent, a tiny distance each year, but over the centuries they reclaimed everything they had lost.

"A few mountaintops and parts of the coast remained free, but otherwise this land was one great forest of birch, pine, oak, ash, maple, and lime, with glades where wild cattle grazed among the flowers. Out of this richness, this teeming forest with its birds and animals, I was born. So much life!"

The Green Man sighed. "All that creation, all that complexity, brought forth a spirit. Likewise, all the death and decay—for such a place has so many brief lives— brought forth its own spirit in balance. Balance, you see, is everything."

"That was the Malifex, wasn't it?" asked Sam.

"Yes, child. That spirit has been called the Malifex. We were two sides of the same coin, as your saying goes—light and dark, life and death—in perfect equilibrium. Then, humans came across the land bridge from Europe." The Green Man fell silent.

"At first," he continued after a while, "it was just one more thread in the tapestry of the forest, more diversity to be celebrated. But humans were different. Humans were intelligent. Through them, through their thoughts, the Malifex and I became aware. We became conscious and knew ourselves and knew that we were opposed. The Malifex moved among the first humans and began to shift the natural balance. Those first humans to come to these islands were simple farmers and brought with them a few plants, the first crops, which they planted in clearings they cut from the forest with stone tools.

"But the Malifex taught them to be greedy, taught them better ways to cut down the forest. Soon, under his guidance, stone tools were replaced by bronze and bronze by iron. As the villages and fields grew, the forest shrank, and with it my power.

"However, there was good in humans as well as evil. They discovered the power that comes from the land, from the web of life, and from the wheel of the seasons. Through long study and the careful garnering of knowledge, the Craft of the Wise was born to protect and celebrate the earth. From among the Wise, a hero arose. His name is now forgotten, but he was one of the first kings of this land and great among the practitioners of the Craft. With his wisdom and love for the earth, he united his people against the forces of darkness and, for a brief time, ruled in peace and harmony with nature.

"So it has been down the ages. The Malifex rises and is

thrown down, the balance of power shifts back and forth, and the wheel turns full circle." The Green Man fell silent.

"And that's it?" demanded Sam after a disbelieving pause. "It all just turns out okay in the end, 'cuz that's how it's always been? Well, I've got news for you—this time it's not going to work. There's no hero—just me. And there's no power for good left out there. There's only pollution, and urban crowding, . . . and . . . and litter, and it stinks. You've got to do something!"

The Green Man looked at him, pale amber eyes in the leaves. "There is always good in the world, child. Balance is everything. The wheel must turn—remember that."

"Oh, how touching," said a familiar voice from across the clearing. "A meeting of minds between my cowardly brother and our pint-sized hero. I surrender!" The Malifex laughed. "I suppose, in light of our location, I could lose the suit." With a wave of his hand, his appearance changed. He became a towering figure in chain mail and black cloth, darkness trailing behind him like wings. An iron helmet enclosed most of his face; a pair of piercing green eyes stared from the eyeholes. In his right hand, he held a long wooden shaft to which he had attached the spearhead stolen from Amergin's grasp. "That feels more comfortable. Just like old times, brother." He spat the final word as if it were venom. "Hmmmm? Oh, I see you've noticed my new toy," he said, following the Green Man's gaze. "Our young friend here kindly retrieved it for me. Yes, brother, the Spear of Destiny, the power to pierce any defense, to change the course of history. Look around you, my foolish sibling—this wood is the last remnant of the old wildwood, your last refuge. You have cowered here for too long, while out there," he gestured vaguely behind him, "out in the real world, my dominion is almost complete. I have ripped the living heart out of your precious land, brother. It lies choked and poisoned, and nothing now can save it."

The Green Man rose to his feet. "Remember, Sam," he said in his strange, musical voice, "the wheel must turn."

"Yes, all very instructional, I'm sure," interrupted the Malifex, "but I grow bored. Nothing personal, brother, but . . . DIE!" And with that word, he hurled the Spear of Destiny with the full force of his malice. It caught the Green Man full in the chest, the spearhead protruding from his back, and he staggered backward, clutching at the shaft. His amber eyes turned to Sam for one last time as he stumbled and fell back on the grass in the center of the stone circle. The Malifex threw back his head in a bellow of triumph, his darkness closed in around him, and he was gone.

Sam sank to his knees on the grass.

chapter 14

Charly moaned and sat up. Looking around her in confusion, she saw Sam on his knees next to an indistinct shape. "Sam?" she called, but there was no response. She went over and knelt beside him. "Was . . . was that him?" she asked.

The body of the Green Man was merging back into the earth. His hair and clothing had mingled with the grass and leaves around him, and his features were blurring like melting wax.

"The Malifex was here," said Sam finally. "He killed him, with the spear I gave him."

Charly put one hand on his shoulder but could think of nothing to say. They knelt there in silence as the body of the Green Man continued to merge with the land.

"Sam," said Charly after a while, "what about the tear? Have you tried the tear?"

Sam turned to her with red eyes. "He's dead! Don't you understand? He's dead, and it's my fault!"

"Sam, just do it for me. Humor me. Do it now, while there's still something of him left." The Green Man was becoming steadily less distinct from the ground around him.

Sam stared at Charly for a moment. "You don't give up easily, do you?"

"I never give up," Charly smiled back at him. Sam went over to the head of the Green Man, drawing the chain from around his neck. He knelt down and placed the tear against the Green Man's forehead, then closed his eyes and tried to reach out with his mind, probing with his senses for a sign of life. For a moment, nothing happened. Then, with a piercing scream, Sam was hurled backward, landing on the grass with the tear still clasped in his hand. An uncontrollable spasm made his back arch, lifting his body clear of the ground, and his eyes rolled back in his head. He gasped a few times through clenched teeth, then collapsed, limp and lifeless on the ground.

Charly rushed to his side, frantically checking his pulse and breathing. He was alive but unconscious, his breathing fast and shallow. She made him as comfortable as possible, placed her rolled-up jacket underneath his head and then, not knowing what else to do, settled down to watch and wait.

The sun, close to its highest point, slowly dropped in the sky as the afternoon wore on, but still Sam showed no sign of life. The shadows of the trees fringing the stone circle lengthened and engulfed them, and Charly fell deeper and deeper into despair.

Sam's plight was her fault—she had insisted that he try the tear. Now she was lost and far from home, and Sam still showed no signs of regaining consciousness. She leaned over his motionless body, humming under her breath as she stroked the hair away from his forehead.

Rocking back and forth, she began to sing, drawing from memory the words to the tune she had been humming. It was something her mother had taught her, something very old, in Gaelic:

Tha mi fo chùram a dhiu ro eileadh
Tha mi fo chùram 's fo mhoran tursa.
'S mo cheist air cùirteir a' bhrollaich ghlè-ghil.
Tha mi fo chùram a dhiu ro eileadh.

As she sang, a single tear ran down her face and dropped on Sam's forehead.

His eyes flickered open, revealing an intense amber color, honey-golden with flecks that glowed like fire. He sat up, and, as he rose, a darkness filled with leaves and twigs rose with him. He climbed to his feet and stood, clothed in greenery and shadow.

His amber eyes turned to Charly. "Thank you," he said in a musical voice. "I think everything is going to be okay now." He took a deep breath and looked around him, then strode over to a patch of tall grass and retrieved the Helm of Herne. As he placed it on his head, the helmet seemed to melt and vanish, leaving just the antlers, which appeared to grow directly from his head.

"What's happened?" asked Charly in a small voice. "Who . . . who are you?"

"I'm still Sam," he replied, "but I'm him, as well—I'm the Green Man, Cernunnos, the Horned God. I'm all those things, and I've got some unfinished business."

Charly looked up at him. He seemed very tall and alien, but he still had Sam's smile as he asked her, "Will you be all right here?"

She nodded. "Yes. Go—do whatever you have to do."

Sam stood for a moment in thought. What had been the body of the Green Man was unrecognizable, a long, green mound, like a barrow. The shaft of the spear, buried in his chest, had taken root and sprouted. A slender young birch tree grew from the top of the mound, marking the center of the stone circle.

Sam cast around him with his new senses. Through the soles of his feet he could feel the slow grind of the earth's crust, tectonic plates groaning in ancient agony as the fires of the planet's core cooled. He felt water rise from the soil and rush through the stems of a million plants, hissing through microscopic tubes before being released into the atmosphere around him. There was a constant background buzz: the sounds of birth and death, the brief lives of bacteria in the soil, the pop and crackle of insects entering and leaving the cycle of life.

He could smell the thoughts of birds and mammals— sparks of attention from a flycatcher on a nearby branch, the hot fire of a weasel's mind as it hunted in the brambles. Charly's thoughts were a mix of concern and fear and something deeper. He tried to look closer but came up against a wall, a dark place where he could not look. The Green Man had said, "She is of the Goddess and therefore beyond my power." Sam left her and sent his mind farther afield.

He caught what he was looking for. A stench of wrong, of evil, faint but increasing the farther out he sent his thoughts. The trail of the Malifex! As he followed it, he realized it was heading toward London. That figured. The heart of his empire was there, the center of his web. He was returning to complete his dominion of the land.

Sam turned and smiled at Charly, then melted into the shadows. He left the ancient wildwood behind him and plunged into the earth as a swimmer dives into water. Shifting from shape to shape, he passed through the landscape like a ghost, riding in the minds of a flock of starlings, running as a fox, flowing with a broad river. "I am the flood across the plain," he thought to himself, and he was a salmon, sleek speckled flanks glistening in the green gloom of a pool. Casting around him, he picked up the taste of the Malifex, a metallic tang of evil on the currents of the water, and with a flick of his tail he moved on.

"I am the hawk above the cliff," he thought, and then he was a peregrine, arrowing through the night on sleek wings. Up and up he flew, until he hung, poised, above the earth. The dying rays of the sun, as it sank beneath the rim of the world, stained his breast like blood. The wind spoke to him then, crying out against the evil of the Malifex, and Sam smelled the stink of him on the air. With a flick of his wings, he plunged back toward the ground and melted into the landscape once more.

In a thousand animal shapes, he crossed the land, mingled with its fabric, resonating to its particular frequency as the night wore on. Wherever he went, the land betrayed the presence of the Malifex, crying out against his touch.

In the silent, graveyard hours of early morning, Sam crested a ridge and stood for a moment in human form, panting, his breath white on the cold air. To the east were the lights of the city of Salisbury in southern England. But ahead was the vast, uninhabited darkness of Salisbury Plain. Beneath his feet he could sense the remains of a Roman road, one of the network of ley lines that criss-crossed the land. He could feel the power flowing into him, as if he were plugged into an energy field.

In the distance, he could see a flare of more intense darkness, like a tornado sweeping across the plain: the Malifex. Dark clouds encircled him, and lightning flick-ered through the gloom. Crackling with power, Sam flowed down the hill and across windswept fields. Ahead he sensed a major beacon of energy, a nexus in the web of ley lines. He cast forward his sight and chuckled.

"Oh, yes," he thought, "that will do." Directly ahead, the beeline of the Malifex's path to London brought him very close to Stonehenge, the ancient circle of stones.

"Malifex!" shouted Sam, "Stop!" The core of darkness ahead ground to a sudden halt. Sam veered to the left, to-ward the looming shadow of Stonehenge, drawing the Malifex after him. Ignoring roads and security fences, Sam headed for the center of the ancient circle and stood, feet braced, waiting. Very soon, a black vortex of energy burst between the standing stones and came to a halt. The spi-raling energy coalesced into the shape of the Malifex, tall and forbidding, cloaked in shadow.

"You?" he snarled. "I thought I killed you."

"I think," replied Sam, "you have me confused with someone else."

"The boy?" rumbled the Malifex, "That's impossible!" He took a few steps forward, peering at Sam in confusion.

Sam said, "I'm starting to think nothing's impossible. For instance, I think I might be able to destroy you."

The Malifex threw back his head and bellowed with laughter. "The greatest heroes of ten millennia have failed to destroy me! And even though you seem to have inherited some of my late brother's tricks, you are, at the end of it all, just a boy."

Sam smiled. "'I am an infant; who but I peeps from the unknown dolmen arch?' Do you think this place could be described as a dolmen?" he asked, gesturing around them at the ancient stone arches.

"That would be stretching it. And what if it could? A line from a piece of appalling doggerel by that fool Amergin—I fail to see the significance."

"Just a thought," sighed Sam. "Anyway, let's get going with this?"

"I will get going," replied the Malifex, "you will die!" He gestured to his right and left, and from between the great stones slunk two black, feline shapes. As they approached Sam, they seemed to writhe and grow, rising up on their hind legs. Sam could make out fangs in wrinkled, batlike faces and piercing green eyes. Wings of darkness fanned the air around them, bringing a sickening stench. They approached from either side, taloned fingers at the ready. Sam realized they had him trapped, the Malifex in front of him and a great slab of stone at his back. With his mind, he reached out to the stone, feeling its crisp mineral vibration, the metallic taste of crystal lattices. He drew on that feeling, pulled it into himself, until he was resonating in tune with it. He felt himself linked to the earth, to the ancient story of the rocks, part of a mineral sphere still cooling from its birth in a cloud of gas around the sun.

With a snarl, the two hideous servants of the Malifex pounced, but Sam was ready. He flung one hand out to each side, catching each of them by the wrist. Where he touched them, their skin turned hard and gray. A grating crackle could be heard as flesh turned into stone. The two creatures howled with rage and thrashed in Sam's grasp, but their rage soon turned to screams of fear. They looked to the Malifex for help, but he stared impassively as his servants fossilized before his eyes. With a last mineral grating noise, the transformation was complete. Sam stood before the Malifex flanked by two new standing stones, shapeless granite monoliths in the center of the ancient circle.

"Oh, very clever," snapped the Malifex. "We have been studying hard, haven't we? Well, it isn't going to ... HELP!" And with that, he drew back one gauntlet-clad fist and hurled a bolt of green energy at Sam. It hit him square in the chest, knocking him back against the stone slab, green sparks crawling like worms over his skin. The Malifex advanced toward Sam, power crackling around him, darkness following after him.

Sam searched frantically for something he could use. He seemed to feel a presence, as if someone was standing behind him, just out of sight. Closing his eyes, he opened his mind and felt the spirit of the Green Man take hold of his perceptions and direct them downward, into the soil. The hard-packed turf of the ancient monument was dry and sparse, and yet it crackled with life. The roots of the grass intertwined with the pale, delicate nets of fungus, through which crawled countless thousands of bacteria.

Sam took a deep breath and opened himself to this sea of life-energy. Where the Malifex took his power by force, Sam merely borrowed, and the land gave freely. A surge of energy traveled up through his legs and hung in his chest, pulsating to the beating of his heart. Pointing both hands at the approaching shadow of the Malifex, Sam released that pent-up energy in a single, crackling blast. The Malifex was hurled backward, hitting the ground with a thud that made the ancient stones rattle. He lay there motionless for a few moments, a sprawled pool of darkness, faint worms of amber light marking the outlines of his helmet and breastplate. Then, like gathering storm clouds, the Malifex rose to his feet.

He bent over Sam and hissed, "This has gone on long enough!" Hands outstretched, fingers clawed, he pumped malevolent energy into Sam's body from both sides. Sam's back arched as green lightning crackled around him. After a time that seemed like eternity, the assault relented, and Sam slumped back onto the rock.

Panting, eyes closed, he groped around with his mind, searching for help, but he was on his own. Despair washed over him, and suddenly he was just a kid, frightened, alone in the dark. No more health bonuses, no more lives. Game over. The knowledge came almost as a relief. After all, how could he ever have been expected to win, when he and the Malifex were drawing on exactly the same power? It was like trying to beat yourself.

This reminded Sam of something the Green Man had

said—that he and the Malifex were two sides of the same coin, that the balance of power shifted back and forth, but a balance was always maintained. Something seemed to crystallize in his mind, pieces slotting into place. The best games, he reflected, always had an element of strategy, of problem solving. In the darkness of his own mind, Sam smiled, and he thought he heard a musical chuckle, like the sound of distant bells.

The Malifex peered down at his motionless form. When his eyes flickered open, the Malifex peered closely into Sam's face. "Why...are...you...not...AFRAID?" he bellowed.

Sam beckoned for him to come closer, then whispered, "I know a secret." He smiled. "Your brother gave me a clue. So did Amergin. There's no darkness without light—you can't destroy the spirit of the Green Man, because you're two sides of the same coin."

"Oh, can't I?" sneered the Malifex. "Let's just put that theory to the test, shall we?" He gathered himself up, tall and dreadful against the sky. Arms outflung, he drew on all the power at his disposal. All the evil and suffering he had created, the misery and destruction he had caused, all this came flooding into him. From the traffic-snarled highways and the derelict factories, from the faceless office blocks and the litter-strewn streets, he soaked up despair. With a scream, he hurled a concentrated blast of blinding green energy at Sam, focused it on his heart, and held it there.

Sam relaxed, slumped back on the stone slab like a sacrificial victim, but still there was a smile on his lips. As the shaft of energy continued to flow into him, he seemed to grow, to become more solid, more massive, as if made of some material far denser than flesh. Leaves spilled from the corners of his mouth and scrambled off into his hair. A green darkness of vegetation spread out around him like a cloak as he rose unsteadily to his feet. The Malifex seemed much smaller now, but still he continued to pour energy into Sam's heart. Sam looked down at him with blazing amber eyes and said, in his rich musical voice, "And that is the other part of the secret. Energy cannot be created or destroyed. It merely flows around the circle, and all is held in balance. As you grew stronger, I grew weaker, and as you empty your power into me, so I grow strong again." The Malifex was a shrunken figure now, the beam of energy he directed at Sam sputtering and dying. "And now let us make an end of this," said Sam, and reached out one hand.

Streamers of darkness began to fray from the form of the Malifex, pouring off into the night in all directions. He began to scream, but as his substance was dispersed the scream dwindled and was gone. Soon Sam stood alone in the center of the circle of Stonehenge, eyes closed. "Goodbye, brother," he sighed, "until next time."

Sam looked around him. He felt bloated with power, crackling with potential, but already he could feel that the spirit of the Green Man would soon depart. He had to do something while he still could, while the power was still with him. He had to put right what the Malifex had made wrong. He cast out his sight, far, far beyond Stonehenge, until he could feel the whole of the land in his mind. He tasted the factory smoke, the polluted rivers, the bitter tang of lead in the air. With an increasing sense of panic, his mind darted around, looking for some sign of hope. Here and there, he sensed tiny remnants of the ancient forest, patches of meadow and heathland, protected as nature reserves and surrounded by the slow creep of housing developments. Farther afield, he found larger areas of beauty and majesty, but everywhere was the tang of acid in the rain and the scars of human activity.

He sent his mind backward, back through the years, watched the sprawl of development recede, watched the choking tide of the Industrial Revolution roll back from the land. Farther and farther back he sent his thoughts, and then he stopped.

Yes, this was what he was looking for, a time of balance, a golden age. The great primeval forest had been pushed back to a remnant of its former glory but still covered huge areas of the wild uplands. In the lowland valleys, small villages nestled at the center of their well-tended fields, and each settlement had its own woodland, carefully managed and treasured as a source of building materials and fuel. In the meadows, the hay was drying in the late summer sun. The hedges and lanes bustled with birds and butterflies. The low, rich fields along the rivers glistened with a web of ditches and drains, where the dragonflies hawked among the irises. This was what he was looking for, a time when light and dark, destruction and creation, seemed to be in careful balance.

He could bring back that time; he had the power. He remembered how Amergin had brought back the land bridge to Old Harry and how he had shown them the procession that took the Helm of Herne to its burial place. He could adapt that technique, bring back an entire age and preserve it, unchanging, in the present.

Then he stopped. The Green Man had said to him, "the wheel must turn—remember that." Sam thought he knew now what that meant. Yes, he could impose this vision of a golden age on the land and hold it there, frozen in time. But all he would do would be to create another museum, something dead, preserved like a fly in amber. The land needed to change, for good or for evil. The circle had to turn.

With a sigh, he brought his thoughts back to the present. His power was starting to slip away, and the spirit of the Green Man would soon be gone. Before that happened, though, Sam sent out his power and freed all those whose minds were ensnared in the web of the Malifex. Throughout the land, people shook their heads, as if waking from an evil dream, and looked at the dawn with fresh eyes.

"There," he thought to himself, "we're on our own, for the time being. Whatever we do now, we do it of our own free will." He turned and headed south, toward Dorset.

Epilogue

Sam took a break from packing and slipped away to Charly's cottage. Uncle Pete seemed back to normal. His parents also seemed none the worse for their experience, although his father in particular seemed kind of dazed. The family vacation seemed to have gone surprisingly quickly, so quickly, in fact, that they seemed to have done hardly anything on his itinerary. He vowed to take a two-week break next time.

Sam knocked on the cottage door. It was answered by Charly's mother.

"Oh, hello, dear," she said, distractedly. "Come on in. Charly's around somewhere."

She bustled off, leaving Sam to close the door behind him. He followed the sound of voices to the study, where Charly and Amergin were laughing.

"Ah, it's our young hero!" exclaimed Amergin. Charly just smiled at him. "And how are you feeling?" Amergin continued.

"Okay, I think," replied Sam. "I . . . well . . . it's difficult to get used to. At first, I felt like I'd gone blind—going from being able to see and feel everything to being, you know, just normal again. Then I sort of got used to it, but now that I've had time to think about it, I don't think I am back to normal."

"Were you ever?" asked Charly.

"It's as if," continued Sam, ignoring her, "a part of the Green Man has been left behind. Sometimes I get the feeling he's standing right behind me or right behind my mind, peering out through my eyes. I seem to be able to see things more clearly, smell things I couldn't smell before . . . " he trailed off, unable to describe the sensation.

"When you have been touched by such a vision, my friend," said Amergin gravely, "you cannot expect to be quite the same ever again."

"How about you?" asked Sam. "How are you feeling?" Amergin jumped to his feet and exclaimed, "Never better! Under the tender care of Megan . . . er . . . your mother," he glanced at Charly, "I seem to have made a complete recovery."

"Complete recovery, my foot!" said Megan, coming into the room. "Don't make the mistake of thinking I'm as crazy as I look. I didn't like to say anything at the time— I'm sure you had your reasons—but you were very obviously pretending to be hurt." Everyone turned to look at Amergin, who looked at his feet.

"Ah," he sighed, "you are a wise woman indeed. Although I did have a rather nasty knock on the head."

"Yes," agreed Megan, "but nothing more. I've done enough healing to know that. I think you owe Sam an explanation."

Amergin looked sheepishly at Sam. "The Malifex constantly made the mistake of underestimating you. He seemed to think that I was his chief threat, so I let him believe that he had put me out of action. He ignored you, which left you free to do what you had to do."

"You just lay there and let me think I was on my own!" Sam exploded. "I was terrified!"

"You wouldn't have gone through with it if you hadn't thought you were the last hope," said Amergin. "Besides, I knew you would be all right."

"What do you mean, you knew?" asked Charly.

"Don't forget," replied Amergin, "I—like our young friend here—once had a glimpse of the whole of creation, and I have a terribly good memory for the little details." He smiled apologetically.

"I think," Charly said, "that Mom's not the only one who's not as crazy as she looks."

"Anyway," Sam sighed, "we've just about finished packing the car. I just came to say good-bye." He turned to Amergin. "Will I see you again?" he asked. "What happens next? Do you have to go back in the barrow?"

Amergin threw back his head and laughed. "My days of sleeping on stone slabs are gone, my friend!" he exclaimed. "The world is stuck with me now."

"I have asked Mr. Wisdom to stay," Megan said with a shy smile at Amergin, "and he's accepted. We've got a lot to talk about." Amergin went to stand by her side and rather awkwardly put an arm around her.

"Oh, come on," said Charly to Sam in disgust, "let's leave them alone." Sam followed her out into the courtyard. "Well," she began, "this is it, I suppose. You did . . . all right."

"Thanks," Sam smiled back, "so did you. Tell me one thing, though. How did you get back here from Dartmoor?"

"Oh, now you start worrying about me!" she exclaimed, remembering being in the ancient clearing and her successful effort to transform herself into a small brown bird. "It's a good thing I wasn't relying on you to bring me back—I'd still be there! Anyway, mind your own business. A girl's got to have some secrets." She suddenly leaned forward and kissed Sam on the cheek.

"Now get going!" she said. "And come back and see us!" Then she turned and ran into the cottage.

Sam stood for a moment, rubbing his cheek in surprise. "Yeah," he said to himself, "I think I will." With that he turned and walked toward the waiting car.

author acknowledgments

I would like to thank all the people who helped with the writing of this book, particularly those friends and relatives who read and commented on early drafts. I would also like to acknowledge the contribution of Jack Todhunter, who started me on this road. My particular thanks, however, go to my wife, Karin, who has acted as unpaid editor, agent, proofreader and—most importantly—keeper of the faith.

about the author

Steve Alton lives in southern England. As well as writing in his spare time, he is a botanical illustrator, a computer graphics artist, and a photographer. This is his first novel.